**When a deadly traitor
threatens to dishonor a top secret agency,
A YEAR OF LOVING DANGEROUSLY
begins....**

Easton "East" Kirby

Strong and powerfully built—and guaranteed to
melt hearts with his mesmerizing brown eyes.

*SPEAR's head honcho wasn't playing fair
when he assigned enticing Agent Alicia Corbin
to bring East Kirby back to the field.
Now, a diabolical maneuver by the traitor
has raised the stakes for East—
making his partnership with Alicia imperative!*

Alicia Corbin

A green-eyed beauty with a body sure to bring even
the strongest man to his knees.

*Her loyalty to SPEAR knew no bounds. But would
she gain the upper hand in this seductive stalemate
with formidable legend Easton Kirby?*

Jonah

Though his identity is top secret, this mystery man
has enough presence and authority to keep his
agents on the alert.

*As the shadowed entity at the helm of SPEAR,
Jonah has a fierce code of honor. He's not about to
let anything—or anyone—bring SPEAR down....*

**Join twelve top agents in their search to
safeguard the country—and lose their hearts to
love—in twelve novels guaranteed to provide you
with A YEAR OF LOVING DANGEROUSLY.**

Dear Reader,

As you have no doubt noticed, this year marks Silhouette Books' 20th anniversary, and for the next three months the spotlight shines on Intimate Moments, so we've packed our schedule with irresistible temptations.

First off, I'm proud to announce that this month marks the beginning of A YEAR OF LOVING DANGEROUSLY, a twelve-book continuity series written by eleven of your favorite authors. Sharon Sala, a bestselling, award-winning, absolutely incredible writer, launches things with *Mission: Irresistible,* and next year she will also write the final book in the continuity. Picture a top secret agency, headed by a man no one sees. Now picture a traitor infiltrating security, chased by a dozen (or more!) of the agency's best operatives. The trail crisscrosses the globe, and passion is a big part of the picture, until the final scene is played out and the final romance reaches its happy conclusion. Every book in A YEAR OF LOVING DANGEROUSLY features a self-contained romance, along with a piece of the ongoing puzzle, and enough excitement and suspense to fuel your imagination for the entire year. Don't miss a single monthly installment!

This month also features new books from top authors such as Beverly Barton, who continues THE PROTECTORS, and Marie Ferrarella, who revisits THE BABY OF THE MONTH CLUB. And in future months look for *New York Times* bestselling author Linda Howard, with *A Game of Chance* (yes, it's Chance Mackenzie's story at long last), and a special in-line two-in-one collection by Maggie Shayne and Marilyn Pappano, called *Who Do You Love?* All that and more of A YEAR OF LOVING DANGEROUSLY, as well as new books from the authors who've made Intimate Moments *the* place to come for a mix of excitement and romance no reader can resist. Enjoy!

Leslie J. Wainger
Executive Senior Editor

Please address questions and book requests to:
Silhouette Reader Service
U.S.: 3010 Walden Ave., P.O. Box 1325, Buffalo, NY 14269
Canadian: P.O. Box 609, Fort Erie, Ont. L2A 5X3

Sharon Sala
MISSION: IRRESISTIBLE

Published by Silhouette Books

America's Publisher of Contemporary Romance

Special thanks and acknowledgment are given
to Sharon Sala for her contribution to the
A Year of Loving Dangerously series.

This book is written in honor of the nameless people
who have dedicated their lives to making my country safe and secure.
Your identities may be unknown, but the sacrifices you have made
have not gone unappreciated. I dedicate this story to you
with the hope that if the favor had to be returned,
we would be strong enough to
withstand and endure.

SILHOUETTE BOOKS

RECYCLED PAPER

ISBN 0-373-27086-0

MISSION: IRRESISTIBLE

Visit Silhouette at www.eHarlequin.com

Printed in U.S.A.

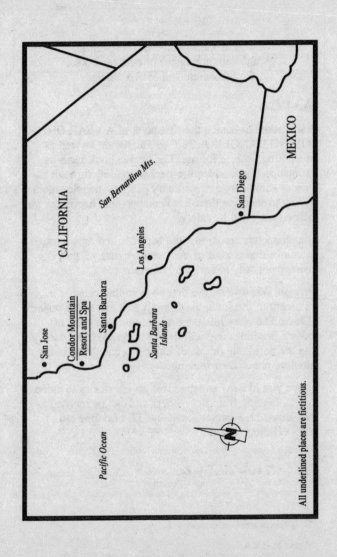

All underlined places are fictitious.

A note from Sharon Sala, bestselling,
award-winning author of over ten books
for Silhouette and MIRA Books:

Dear Reader,

Being asked to launch the first book of A YEAR OF
LOVING DANGEROUSLY was an honor, as well as
an exciting venture for me. The twelve-book series is
a romance-filled, adventure-packed journey through the
lives of some very extraordinary people—people who are
willing to sacrifice their lives and personal happiness for
their country and its safety.

The characters are strong and heroic, often drawn into
situations that are out of their control, and yet they
manage not only to survive, but triumph.

Mission: Irresistible, the first book in the series, is a
testament to the strength of family ties and to the power
of love. The story line is an all-too-familiar echo of
today's headlines and will draw you quickly and deeply
into the unfolding drama of innocents caught up in a
situation not of their making.

I hope you like my story, as well as the stories to come.
I enjoy hearing from my readers and can be reached at
P.O. Box 127, Henryetta, OK 74437, or online c/o
www.eHarlequin.com.

Sharon Sala

Prologue

The American flags above the tall man's head popped smartly as the hot July breeze whipped them into a frenzy; colorful reminders of a nation's gratitude for the dedication and sacrifices of countless soldiers over the centuries who had kept the country free.

But gratitude was the last thing on the man's mind as he stood before the black, polished surface of the Vietnam War Memorial. The petals of the rose that he carried were beginning to droop, but it hardly mattered. The man for whom it was meant had long ceased to care for anything of this earth.

It wasn't the first time he'd been here on the nation's birthday, so the unusual number of visitors did not surprise him. Yet as he moved through the people, he was struck by the silence of so large a crowd.

The memorial in itself was an emotionally moving sight. A seemingly endless stretch of gleaming black marble with nothing but names etched upon its surface. Names of fathers and of sons, of brothers and of uncles, of friends and neighbors who'd given their lives because their country had asked it of them.

His heart swelled painfully as he began to scan the surface. It was here—somewhere near the center and about a third of the way down. He stepped around a small, stoop-shouldered woman, then in front of a young couple with two small children, his gaze centering on the names. The farther he walked, the harder his heart began to pound. And then suddenly he stiffened.

There it was: Frank Wilson.

He traced the letters of the name with his forefinger. By the time he got to the last letter he was looking at the world through a blur and all he could think was, *Damn you.*

His jaw clenched and a muscle jerked at the side of his temple as he dropped the rose at the base of the wall and turned to walk away. As he did, the wind gusted, causing the flags to flutter, and ruffling the streaks of gray at the temples of his short, dark hair. He squinted against the sunlight and dropped a pair of sunglasses in place as he moved toward the grassy area beyond. But the sound of the blowing flag became mixed with the memories in his mind, turning from wind and heat to the rapid fire of machine guns, the unforgettable thunder of landing helicopters and the nightmare that was Vietnam.

Saigon 1974

It had been raining off and on all day and the clothes the girl on the street corner wore were plastered to her skin until it looked as if she was wearing nothing at all. She put her hands under her breasts and lifted them toward the trio of American soldiers coming down the street.

"Hey G.I., wanna party? Good sex…hot sex…five dolla'."

Private Joseph Barone of Brooklyn, New York whistled beneath his breath and elbowed his buddy.

"Oowee, Davie boy, would you look at her. You want to get yourself a little of that?"

The thought of a physical release within the warmth of a woman's arms was strong, but David Wilson had seen past her painted face and skimpy clothes to the child beneath and cringed. He wasn't the only one out of his element. She was doing all she knew, trying to survive in a world gone mad and adding to her hell seemed impossible to consider. Instead of telling the truth, that having sex with a fourteen-year-old whore turned his stomach, he used sarcasm instead.

"Do I want a little of what? The clap?" David drawled.

Joe Barone laughed and slapped his buddy on the back. "It might be worth it, kid."

David gave her one last glance and then shook his head. "You and Pete go on, though. I'll meet you back at the barracks."

They laughed at his reticence and pivoted sharply, heading back to the woman before another one of their compatriots beat them to the offer.

David shoved his hands in his pockets and hunched his shoulders as he moved along the crowded sidewalk. An old man sat cross-legged on the ground, hawking his wares in a sing-song litany while dangling a plucked fowl above his head in an effort to catch a buyer's eye. David's nose wrinkled in protest to the smell as he passed and wondered how long the man had been trying to sell that particular bird.

He turned the corner, fully intent upon heading for the barracks, when he heard a familiar laugh. He turned, a look of expectancy on his face. He'd know that laugh anywhere. It was his brother, Frank.

He pivoted sharply, searching the constantly moving masses for sight of his brother's face. If he could hook up with Frank, it would be a good way to pass the afternoon. His eyes were alight as he began to scan the crowd.

Frank was his elder by four years and the single reason David was in Vietnam. Lying about his age to sign up had been simple. It was the fact that he and his brother had wound up in the same company that was amazing. But David was glad. Frank had always been more than just a big brother. He'd been a substitute father—a playmate—and when he wasn't thumping on David's head himself, a bodyguard in the rough neighborhood in which they'd grown up.

The crowd in front of David parted suddenly to let a man with a pushcart pass by and as it did, he saw his brother in the distance. At that same moment, he realized Frank wasn't alone. He paused, staring curiously at the pair with whom Frank was conversing. Their heads were close together, as if they didn't want to be overheard. And when one of them straightened and turned, staring directly toward David, he found himself ducking into a doorway instead of hailing them as he'd intended. There was something about the men that he didn't trust. He watched a bit longer, trying to remember where he'd seen them, and as he did, it sud-

denly hit him. A few months back, one of his buddies had pointed them out in a nightclub as being Dutch. When David had asked why two men from Holland would be here in the middle of such hell, his buddy had laughed and said, commerce, Davie-boy, commerce. It had taken a while before David realized they were suspected gunrunners.

Now, as he watched, Frank grinned and slapped one of the men on the back, then shook his hand. When he did, David's gut began to knot. Why would Frank be talking to men like that? Like everyone else, he knew it was men like that who were responsible for selling American-made weapons to the Vietcong. Men from other countries who were in this strictly for the money, who had no allegiance to a nation, not even their own. Immediately he thought of the money Frank had been flashing during the past two months. Money he claimed he had won playing cards. But Frank was a lousy card player. Always had been. When the men began to move, David followed at a distance, desperate to assure himself that what he was thinking couldn't be true.

It started to rain again, and as it did, the streets began to clear as people took shelter inside the shops or made their way home. In an effort to remain unobserved, David had to stay far behind and twice he thought he'd lost them, only to turn a corner and see the back of Frank's head in the distance.

By the time they reached the outskirts of the city, David's gut was in knots. He'd long ago given up on this being an innocent meeting, and when they slipped into an isolated hut, David groaned inwardly. By the time he reached the hut, the rain had turned to a downpour, smothering all sound save that of the hammer of

*his own heartbeat and the sound of rain on the wet
thatched roof.*

*He moved closer to the door, then shifted so that he
could see inside. The interior was small and gloomy,
yet light enough for David to see an envelope pass
between Frank and the men.*

*No, David thought, and held his breath, watching as
Frank counted the money then slipped it inside his shirt
before handing over a small slip of paper. Without
thinking of the consequences, he stalked into the hut.*

*To say Frank Wilson was stunned, would have been
an understatement, but his shock quickly turned to anger when he realized his little brother had seen it all.
To make it worse, the other men were already drawing
their weapons.*

*"Don't!" he yelled. "He's my brother." Then he
turned to David, fear mixing with guilt. "What the hell
do you think you're doing?"*

*David quickly moved, putting himself between Frank
and the men and yanking the money out of Frank's
shirt and throwing it on the ground.*

*"Saving your stupid ass," he said. "Now let's get
out of here."*

*"What the hell's going on?" one of the men mut-
tered, and waved his gun in Frank Wilson's face.*

*"Leave this to me," Frank said, and shoved David
aside as he began to pick up the money.*

*David stepped on a wad of money just as Frank
reached for it, and in doing so, stepped on Frank's
fingers instead. Pain fueled Frank's rage as he bolted
to his feet, slamming David against the wall of the hut.
Both of the gunrunners aimed their weapons as they
realized their assignation was not as secretive as
they'd wished.*

Frank knew that now both he and David were in trouble. He pulled his own weapon, aiming it at the shorter one's head.

''Don't do it!'' he yelled, and then fired off two shots before the men could answer.

Through the roar of the rain, the sounds were little more than muffled thumps. David was shaking, stunned by his brother's lack of emotion, only to find that Frank had a gun aimed at his face.

''What the hell are you doing?'' David whispered.

''The question should be, what are you going to do about what you just saw?'' Frank countered.

David swallowed. He'd seen that look on his brother's face before.

''What did I see?'' David asked. ''What did you sell them?''

Frank grinned. ''A little steel. A little wood. A little lead. Just natural resources.''

David's skin crawled. ''Guns? You're selling our own guns to the enemy? How can you do that? How can you be a traitor to your own country?''

Frank sneered. ''My own country, as you so fondly call it, sent me over here to die. And I'm not even sure I believe in what I'm fighting for. Why shouldn't I get something out of it besides a coffin?''

David held out his hand. ''Please Frank. Let's just go. No one has to know we were even here. They'll find the bodies and the money, and assume the men killed each other.''

Frank's smile hardened as he dug through one of the dead men's pockets for the slip of paper with the information he'd just sold. When he found it, he wadded it into a very small ball, then popped it in his mouth *like candy, chewed it and swallowed while David looked on in horror.*

"I'm not leaving the money," Frank growled. "It's mine. Now the problem remains, are you gonna snitch?"

"Why? Are you going to kill me, too?"

In Frank's defense, it had to be said that he hesitated, but there was a dark gleam in his eyes when he answered.

"If I have to."

David stared into the barrel of the gun, unable to believe that his fate in life was to come all this way across the world only to be killed by his brother's hand.

"You've gone crazy," David pleaded. "Is this what you really want?"

"What I want, is to be rich," Frank said, and took aim.

Everything afterward seemed to happen in slow motion. Frank's shot searing the back of David's shoulder as he dove for a dead man's gun. Pulling the trigger as he rolled. The water leaking through the roof and falling on his left cheek at the same moment that Frank staggered and fell. The smell of gunpowder and mud as David crawled to his feet. Standing motionless beneath the leak in the roof while the raindrops mixed with tears, then throwing his head back and letting out a gut-wrenching roar of anguish.

Time passed. The rain had stopped. People were moving about and it was only a matter of time before someone found them, and yet David couldn't bring himself to move. It was the sound of a Huey flying overhead that brought him out of his trance.

He staggered to an alcove at the back of the room,

dragged out a can of gasoline and began scattering it all over the walls and then the floor, making sure that the men and the money were saturated as well. Then he moved to the doorway, cautiously peering out. No one was in sight. Unable to look at his dead brother's face, he struck a match and gave it a toss, slipped out of the hut and ran.

He never looked back.

"Here you go Mister."

Startled by the sound of an unfamiliar voice, David Wilson jerked, and the memories sank back into the hell that was his past. He looked down at the young man before him, and at the handful of miniature American flags he was carrying.

"You're a vet, aren't you?" the kid asked.

David hesitated, then shrugged. Admitting that much posed no threat. He nodded.

The kid beamed. "I knew it! I can tell. My dad's a vet. He fought in Desert Storm." Then he pulled a flag from the bunch in his hand and thrust it into the man's palm. "Take it, Mister. You earned it."

David's fingers curled around the small, wooden staff as the kid disappeared. He stared at the colors so long that they began to run together in his mind. When he finally looked up, the glitter in his eyes was no longer moisture and the cut of his jaw was set and firm.

Earned it? He hadn't earned anything but a heartache and a tombstone in Arlington Cemetery. To become the man he was now, he'd had to die, presumably in the line of duty. But nevertheless, David Wilson was dead. The man he'd become was a solitary man. He had no one he could call friend, no identity that mattered, no ties to a community or church. A faceless man

who, some years back had sworn, once again, to give
his life for his country.

Now, they called him Jonah and only two people on
the face of the earth knew his real identity. As the
anonymous director of SPEAR, the most elite counterespionage team ever to be assembled on behalf of the
United States of America, Jonah lived life in the shadows, communicating with his operatives when necessary by coded messages, a cassette delivered with an
order of pizza, cryptic telegrams, and occasionally,
nothing more than a voice on the phone.

SPEAR, first founded by Abraham Lincoln himself
during the Civil War, was an acronym for Stealth, Per-
severance, Endeavor, Attack and Rescue. It was an organization that existed in the shadows of society, and
its existence, the best kept secret in the free world.
Headed throughout the years by mysterious men
known only as Jonah, the succession of Jonahs who
had given their lives to their country were the unre-
cognized heroes of the past. To the world, they were
dead. If they lived long enough to retire, they were
given an entirely new identity and left to face their
twilight years alone, without benefit of old friends or
family.

In a few years, he, too, would retire and another
Jonah would step into his shoes. *Dying* for his country
had seemed an odd sort of justice, considering the fact
that he'd taken his only brother's life.

He watched the kid running across the greens, trying
to remember if he'd ever been that innocent. He then
snorted beneath his breath and shoved the flag into his
pocket and started toward his car. There was no place
in his life for sentiment or regret.

Those years of retirement were, however, looming

closer than he might have liked. Someone was trying to ruin him. Someone wanted him branded a traitor in the very worst way, and despite his access to even the most classified of records, he had been unable to find even a trace of a guilty party. It was, without doubt, the worst thing that had happened to him since Vietnam. It could be anyone, even a disgruntled operative at SPEAR who, by some stroke of fate, had discovered his identity. He was at the point of admitting he needed help, that doing this alone was no longer an option. But there was a problem. He didn't know who to trust.

Chapter 1

One week later: The Northern California coast.

A pair of seagulls perched on the railing surrounding the large, flagstone terrace of the Condor Mountain Resort and Spa. The view, like the resort, was a magnificent complement to the area overlooking the Pacific. The gulls gave an occasional flap of their wings as they squawked between themselves in bird speak while keeping watch for a dropped bit of someone's breakfast pastry. Waiters moved among the tables serving coffee and juice, while others carried freshly made foods to the hot-and-cold buffet that was set up near the door. The idle chatter of the guests as they breakfasted was diluted by the soft breeze and the wide open spaces.

It was an idyllic scene, typical for the resort, but there was nothing typical about Easton Kirby, the man who ran it. Tall and powerfully built, he looked more like a professional athlete than a business man. His shoulders strained against the soft knit texture of his white Polo shirt while navy slacks accentuated the length of leg and muscle. His hair was a shade lighter than his tan, and more than one female guest at the hotel had commented about his resemblance to the actor, Kevin Costner, although his nose had more of a Roman shape to it after having twice been broken. He often smiled, but there were shadows within the glitter of his eyes that congeniality could not disguise. He was a man who lived with secrets he would never be able to share and being a former operative for SPEAR was secondary to the fact that he considered himself a murderer.

That it had happened in the line of duty during a high-speed chase had not cleared his conscience. The teenager who'd come out of nowhere on a bicycle and right into the path of East's oncoming car had been a boy in his prime, having just won a four-year scholarship to a prestigious college, and an honor student throughout his high school years. The headphones he'd been wearing had blocked out the sound of the oncoming cars, and according to the police who'd investigated the accident, he had also bicycled across the highway from the hill above without even trying to stop, obviously trying to beat the traffic. Despite East having been cleared of wrongdoing, the guilt of the act was a hair shirt on his soul. What was done, was done. The kid was dead. End of story.

Afterward, it had been all East could do not to put a gun to his own head. Night after night he kept reliving the sight of the young man's face spotlighted in his headlights, then the impact of flesh against metal and the scent of burning rubber as he'd tried to stop.

SPEAR had sent him through counseling, then to Condor Mountain to rehabilitate. But it didn't take. For three months he had lived in the room that they'd given him, refusing to interact with anyone except on a need-to basis, hiking the mountains at night and trying to purge his soul. And then one dark night during one of his nightly forays, he met Jeff. Fourteen years old and a professional runaway from the welfare system, the kid was as hard and wild as they came. East was drawn to the youth in spite of himself, recognizing the boy's sullen anger as a result of fear rather than meanness. The bond they formed was slow, but it surprised them both. Within a year, Easton Kirby had a whole new role in life. At the age of twenty-five, he became a father to a fourteen-year-old boy, and Jeff was no longer homeless.

A short while later, SPEAR named East manager of the hotel where he'd been sent to recuperate. His file at SPEAR was purged and his days as a counterespionage agent were over. But that hadn't ended his ties with the organization. Condor Mountain Resort and Spa was a part of the Monarch Hotel Chain—a legitimate corporation owned and operated by SPEAR, and available to agents on the verge of burnout.

Occasionally East saw acquaintances from his days of active duty, but only if they were sent to the Condor Resort for some R and R after the close of a particularly grueling case. Yet the tie that had bound them together before had been severed by time and distance. That part of his life was over. He existed in a come-and-go world with his adopted son as his only family and it was just the way he liked it. Only now and then was he haunted by nightmares, and when he was, he focused instead on the doctor Jeff was studying to become, rather than the horrors of his own past. It should have been enough, but the absence of a woman in his life often left him with a rootless, empty feeling. Yet how could he live his own life to the fullest when he'd taken the life of an innocent man?

The two seagulls which been sitting on the railing took flight as a waiter walked past. A few moments later, Easton Kirby walked out on the patio, causing more than a few female hearts to flutter, as well. He nodded and smiled as he moved through the area, but his focus was on the couple at the far table. They'd checked in last night after he'd gone to bed, but his staff had informed him they were here. He made it a habit to personally greet all honeymooners, and from the way the pair was cuddling through their morning meal, their stay at Condor Mountain was off to a good start. He couldn't help thinking how blessed they were. Their whole lives were ahead of them, while his was stalled in a guilt-ridden limbo.

Before he reached their table, his cell phone rang. He moved to a guest-free area of the patio to take the call.

"Hello."

"Kirby."

It had been years since East had heard that voice, but there was no mistaking it. Instinctively, he moved off the terrace and down the steps toward the beach, putting distance between himself and the rest of the world.

"Jonah?"

"Yes."

East reached the first landing, and sat. Something told him he needed to be immobile when he took this call.

"How have you been?" Jonah asked.

East's belly knotted. "Fine, but I'm assuming you know that, sir, or you wouldn't be calling."

A slow intake of breath was all East heard. He waited for Jonah to continue. Chit-chat was not something one did with this man. Finally, Jonah spoke.

"I need to ask a favor of you,"

East's eyes widened. Favor? Jonah didn't ask favors, he gave orders.

"Sir?"

"I have a problem—a big problem," Jonah said. "Someone is trying to destroy me."

East's heart skipped a beat and he stood abruptly, as if bracing himself for an unspeakable blow.

"Destroy you?"

"It's complicated," Jonah said. "Suffice it to say that things are surfacing within high places that make it look as if I'm a war criminal, as well as a traitor to my country." There was a moment of hesitation before he continued. "It's not true."

East's eyes narrowed. "Telling me that was unnecessary. That much I know."

Again, there was a hesitation, then Jonah spoke. "I thank you for that. But the problem still exists and despite my unlimited…uh, shall we say access…to confidential material, I have been unable to trace the source. For all I know, it could be within SPEAR itself."

East was incredulous. "No sir! I don't believe that's possible."

"I would like to think so, too," Jonah said. "But at this point, nothing or no one can be ruled out."

East frowned. "If that's so, then why call me?"

"Because, technically, you are inactive. It's been ten

years since you've been in the field. We have no axes to grind and no issues that could be a possible basis for these actions. I have to trust someone. You're it.''

East's gut knotted tighter. ''Sir…don't ask this of me.''

Jonah's sigh whispered through East's conscience like a knife.

''It's been ten years since that incident with the kid,'' Jonah said.

East swallowed harshly, then closed his eyes against the glare of sunlight upon the water.

''Tell that to my psyche,'' he growled. ''Besides, I have a family to consider.''

''Yes…Jeff, isn't it? Studying to be a doctor?''

''Yes, sir. He's interning now in L.A.''

''He's a man, Kirby, not a kid.''

A noise on the beach below caught Kirby's attention, he opened his eyes and turned. It was a pair of sea lions sunning themselves on an outcropping of rock. For a moment, he lost himself in the spray of surf hammering against the rocks and the seabirds doing a little two-step upon the sand. The urge to take the phone and toss it into the water, disconnecting himself from both Jonah and the world was overwhelming, but it was a futile thought. He'd learned long ago that no matter how hard he'd tried, he had not been able to get away from his past.

''Kirby…are you there?''

East sighed. ''Yes, sir. I was just thinking.''

There was a note of eagerness in Jonah's voice. ''And?''

''I have to ask you a question,'' East said.

''Ask.''

''Is this an order?''

This time, there was no mistaking the sigh in Jonah's voice. "I can't order you to do a personal favor for me."

"I'm not the man I used to be. I've been out of the business too long. I've lost the edge needed to survive."

There was a long moment of silence, then Jonah spoke. "So…you're turning me down."

"Yes."

Again Jonah hesitated, but this time his voice was void of emotion.

"I understand. Oh, and Kirby, this call never happened."

"What call, sir?"

The line went dead and Kirby knew there would never be a traceable record of the call ever happening. A fresh wave of guilt hit him head-on.

"Damn it to hell."

He spun on his heels and headed back to the hotel.

Chapter 2

Sweat slipped from the sweatband around Alicia Corbin's head and into her right eye as she focused on a spot upon the wall in front of her, rather than the pain of burning muscles in her legs. Gripping the handlebars of the workout bike a little tighter, she glanced at the digital readout on the machine and grimaced. Only another mile to go and she could quit.

Although she was a health club regular, she hated working out. Her preference would have been to take a long, leisurely walk in a deeply wooded area with only squirrels and deer for companions rather than some of these perspiring males who kept strutting from one machine to the other, and whose sole intent was for a perfect body and some female adulation. But then Ally would be the first to admit that she was uncomfortable with her own sexuality. She didn't see herself as others saw her. She looked in a mirror and saw a woman on the verge of being too thin, whereas most women would have been overjoyed to be built in her image. Of average height, Ally's slim, finely toned body was strong and high-breasted with hips that would never spread. The striking combination of auburn hair and green eyes gave her youthful features a pixie appearance, rather than that of a sultry vixen. But there was nothing fey about Ally. No one would ever have guessed that she was a highly-trained operative within a secret branch of the government, or that her IQ was off the scale. She'd entered high school at the age of ten, graduating two years later. By the time she had turned seventeen, she had a Ph.D. in physics, another in criminology, and was considering another round of classes when she'd been recruited by SPEAR. At the time, it had seemed like a good idea. Her parents, intellectuals who were more concerned with their life paths than with hers, had left most of her upbringing to hired help and higher education, so it was no jolt for Ally to go from a college campus to the training ground of SPEAR.

But being so much younger than her fellow students at college had been a drawback socially. She had made no close friends. If anyone had happened to notice that the quiet little genius was no longer on campus, it was so much the better. At least she wouldn't be ruining the grading curve for anyone else.

And for Ally, joining SPEAR was all a matter of readjusting priorities. There wasn't much SPEAR's instructors could teach her in the way of technology, but learning about covert activities and enduring the intense physical training put her in an entirely different world. There had been days when she wasn't sure she would survive, yet she had. Now it was so much a part of her life, she rarely thought about the way it had been before.

Today was only the second day of a much needed vacation and making the decision to go to the gym had come in a weak moment. Now, as she neared the end of her workout, the muscles in her legs were weak and burning. She gritted her teeth and bared down on the pedals, giving up her last bit of energy. Just as the digital readout clicked over to read twenty miles, she began to ease off, letting her muscles adjust to stopping. Finally, as she let her feet slip out of the pedals, she slumped over the handlebars with sweat pouring down her neck and between her breasts, her heart thundering in her ears.

As she sat, her cell phone began to ring. Wearily, she slid off the bicycle seat and walked toward the bench where she'd left a fresh towel and her phone, wondering as she did, who could have possibly known she was here. As she picked it up to answer, she remembered she'd left Call Forwarding on her phone.

"Hello?"

"Alicia, we haven't heard from you in a while."

The cool, almost impersonal tone in her mother's voice had long since ceased to hurt her. She draped the fresh towel around her neck and began mopping perspiration as she dropped onto the bench.

"I've been…gone," Ally said, hesitating on the last word. There was never any option about discussing the cases she worked on with anyone, parent or no. In fact, discussion about SPEAR was nonexistent, because to the general public, SPEAR did not even exist.

"We assumed as much." Then, as if it was no big deal, Mavis Corbin added, "Next week is your birthday, but your father and I are going to be out of the country. So, Happy Birthday, Alicia and many more.''

Ally ignored a quick surge of disappointment. It wasn't the first time this had happened. It wouldn't be the last.

''Thank you, Mother,'' Ally said. ''Where are you going this time?''

''Egypt. A whole new burial ground has been discovered. Your father is so excited. This is very important to us, you know.''

Ally grinned bitterly. She knew all too well what was important to her parents and she was low on the list. ''Yes, Mother, I know. Have a good trip and thanks for calling.''

''You're welcome, dear. Take care.''

Before Ally could respond, the line went dead. She hung up the receiver and headed for the showers. She had a sudden urge for a milkshake and a chocolate doughnut. Instead, a half hour later she was standing in line, waiting for her order of black coffee and a plain bagel to be filled.

''Four-fifty,'' the clerk said, handing her a white sack with the top neatly folded and a steaming cup of coffee.

She paid, stuffed her change in the pocket of her sweatpants and headed for the door. It wasn't until she was unlocking her car and the sack bumped against the door that she realized there was something more than a bagel inside. The hair crawled on the back of her neck as she slid behind the steering wheel and locked herself in. Then she set her coffee cup in the holder on the dash and opened the sack.

The small black cassette in the bottom of the sack could only mean one thing.

"Well, hell," Ally muttered, as she slid the cassette into the stereo on the dash. Jonah's deep, gravelly voice was familiar, as was the unusual way in which she'd been contacted. It was typical of the anonymity of SPEAR. Ordinarily she would have been excited about a new assignment, but she hadn't even been home long enough to do laundry or have an all-night session watching her favorite movies.

She started the car, listening to the tape as she drove toward home, every now and then allowing herself a frown as she pinched off bites of the bagel and poked them into her mouth.

As far as assignments went it was unusual, although she couldn't find fault with the location. She'd heard of the spa on Condor Mountain and had no problem at all taking advantage of some free R and R. And Easton Kirby, who was now the manager of the place, was a legend within the agency. Her curiosity piqued as Jonah's spare remarks began to sink in. If she understood him correctly, and she was certain she did because Jonah was not a man to leave anything to the imagination, Jonah needed Easton Kirby on active duty and Kirby had refused. The tape ended with a final order.

Ally was to change his mind—in any way that she could.

She ejected the tape and tossed it back into the sack, well aware that within thirty seconds of it having been played, it would go blank, leaving no trace of ever having been recorded upon. She pulled into the driveway of her house and punched the garage door opener. Her cheeks were flushed, her eyes snapping angrily as she waited for the garage door to go up.

"Change his mind?" she muttered, her voice drip-

ping with sarcasm. "And how am I supposed to do
that...drive him mad with my womanly wiles?"

Seconds later she pulled into the garage, lowered the
door and then got out, but only after the door was completely shut. Her house key was in her hand as she
swept the garage with a casual gaze before making a
move toward the door. Once inside, she dumped her
sweaty gym clothes on the washer and the bagel sack
in the trash, then downed the last of her coffee before
adding the empty cup to the lot.

The red light on her answering machine was blinking, but her mind was on the new assignment. What in
blazes did one wear to coerce a reluctant operative back
into the fold?

Almost a week later and a year older, Ally pulled
into the parking lot of the Condor Mountain Resort and
Spa, then sat for a moment, staring at the magnificence
of the building and grounds. The four-story mixture of
Gothic and Victorian architecture seemed to fit the
starkness of the geography. Lush was not a word that
described this part of the California coast. The moun-
tainous area of the region had steep, and often narrow,
winding roads, and the forestation of the area was
sparse, often leaving bare spots in the rocky terrain.
But there was a beauty to the land that seemed to fit
the power of the waters that pounded the coast. Overhead, seagulls dipped and swooped, riding the air currents while searching for food, and she could hear the
harsh, guttural barks of sea lions coming from the
beach below. From where she was sitting, she could
see the beginnings of a long, descending series of steps
leading down the side of the hill toward the Pacific.
The view was breathtaking and the weather sunny and

breezy, which was typical for this time of year. She couldn't help wishing this was going to be a "real" vacation and not another undercover assignment.

As she got out of the car and went around to the trunk to get her bags, she had to admit, her job this time was hardly on a par with what she normally did. At least she wouldn't be posing as some wayward teenager or wild child in order to infiltrate some crime syndicate. All she had to do was convince Easton Kirby to come back on active duty. How difficult could that be?

She popped the trunk on her car and leaned in to get out her bag. As she did, a large shadow suddenly passed between her and the sun and she knew she was no longer alone. She straightened and turned, expecting a bellhop, or at the least an employee of the resort.

It was a man.

He was tall, so tall, and standing close—too close.

Slightly blinded from the sunlight behind him, she saw nothing but his silhouette. And then he stepped to one side to reach for her bag and she saw his face.

It was Easton Kirby himself—the man she'd come to meet.

Well, this makes it easy. At least I won't have to wangle an introduction.

"Ms. Corbin, welcome to Condor Mountain," he said, as he lifted her bag from the trunk of her car.

She thought nothing of the fact that he would know her on sight. The agency would have followed procedure and notified him ahead of time that an operative would be arriving.

"Thank you," Ally said, a little disconcerted by his height and the way he was looking at her.

She was five inches over five feet tall and he seemed

a good foot taller. And, there was a look in his eyes that made her shiver. She shrugged off the thought that he would know why she'd come, telling herself that it was guilt that was making her nervous.

"This is certainly wonderful service. I only just arrived."

"I know," he said softly, then looked her straight in the eyes. "I was waiting for you."

Ally's lips parted in shock. But only a little and only for a brief moment. As she followed him up the steps and into the hotel, she couldn't shake the notion that he wasn't the only one who'd been waiting. She had a desperate feeling that she'd been waiting for him, too— all of her life.

Oh fine, she thought. Now is not the time for my stifled hormones to kick in. Just because he's sexy, and good-looking, and I'm supposed to talk this man into something he doesn't want to do, doesn't mean I have to complicate this more than it already is.

They reached the registration desk. Before she could speak, he was bypassing it and leading her toward the elevators.

"You're already checked in," he said. "Follow me. I'll show you to your room."

The doors opened and they stepped inside. She watched as he stuck a key into a slot and gave it a turn. Immediately the elevator car started to ascend. She grabbed on to the railing to steady herself, then noted that they had bypassed the fourth floor.

"I thought this hotel only had four floors. Where are we going? Heaven?"

For the first time since her arrival he looked at her and grinned and her heart dropped right to her toes. *Oh lordy. I am so out of my league.*

"No, but some people tend to think the view might be similar," he said. "There's a penthouse suite on the ocean side of the hotel that's not visible from the front entrance. It's reserved for special guests such as yourself."

"Oh," she said, and then looked down at her feet so that he might not see the remorse she was feeling. He was being nice to her because he thought she was over the edge. Slipping. Burned-out. All the adjectives one might use to describe a SPEAR operative on the verge of a breakdown.

He looked at her then, reading her sudden silence as having been reminded of something terrible that must have happened to her on the job and remembered that when SPEAR operatives were ever sent here, it was usually for mental healing.

"Sorry," he said. "I didn't mean to bring up bad memories."

"No, it wasn't that," she began, but the car had stopped and the doors were opening and Easton Kirby was already on the move. She followed, kicking herself for not knowing how to draw men into casual conversation.

They exited into what appeared to be a large foyer. East punched in a series of numbers on the security panel beside the door and then turned the knob.

"Your home away from home," he said, leading the way inside. "I hope your stay will be comfortable." He set her suitcase down in the bedroom, then handed her the key and a card. "The security code is written on the back. My number is on the front. If you need anything at any time of the night or day, all you have to do is call me."

She took the key and the card and slipped them into her pocket. "Thank you, Mr. Kirby."

"You're welcome, Ms. Corbin, and please…call me East."

"If you'll call me Ally, it's a deal," she said, offering her hand.

When he took it, she felt as if she'd been treading water all of her life and someone had just offered her a line to safety. This womanly, helpless feeling was so foreign to Ally that she didn't know how to react.

"Well then," she said, quickly releasing his hold. "Now that we're supposed to be friends, does this mean I don't have to tip you?"

East threw back his head and laughed. A deep-from-the-belly kind of laugh that sent shivers up Ally's spine. She grinned, pleased that she'd gotten some sort of positive response from him.

Still chuckling, East shook his head. "No, you don't have to tip me and we start serving dinner around seven. The restaurant stays open until midnight so remember, if you need anything…"

"Yes, I know," she said, patting her pocket where she'd put his card. "I'll use Ma Bell to reach out and touch."

His smile stilled as he gave her a dark, unreadable look.

"Touching is good," he said quietly, and headed for the door, leaving Ally to put her own interpretation on what he'd just said.

A shudder racked her as she watched him leave. What on earth had she gotten herself into? Then she gritted her teeth and headed for her suitcase. The least she could do was unpack. There were a good four hours of daylight left and a beach to explore.

Something told her that this operation was going to take time. Easton Kirby didn't strike her as malleable. As she went to the closet with an armful of clothes, she couldn't help wondering why Jonah hadn't just ordered this man back to active service. What sort of scenario could possibly have occurred that Jonah would allow a man's personal life to interfere with his duty?

As East was dressing for dinner, he caught himself thinking of Ally Corbin again. It wasn't the first time it had happened since her arrival, and something told him it wouldn't be the last. There was something about her that intrigued him. She was such a mixture of contradictions. Naive, yet tough. He knew what it took to become an agent for SPEAR, so he respected that her skills equaled his own. Yet there was an innocence about her that surprised him. He had no way of knowing that naivete came in not knowing herself. She was beyond book smart, but she didn't have the vaguest idea of how to live a normal life. She'd never been in love, she'd never even made love. Had he known, it might have changed his attitude completely. But all he saw was a beautiful and intriguing young woman who had endured and survived, and was here to heal.

He debated with himself about wearing a tie, then decided against it, opting for the casual look. For some reason, his mind slipped to Jonah, wondering if he'd found someone else to help him out. It had been a week since he'd gotten the call, and he hadn't slept well one night since. Then he reminded himself that was part of his past and he couldn't let it matter.

With a last glance in the mirror, he grabbed his sport coat and exited his apartment. It was time to make an appearance in the dining room.

The Condor Resort ran on schedules, not unlike those of a cruise ship, and sitting at the captain's table, or in this case the manager's, was considered an honor. It was something the previous manager had instigated and East had simply followed suit. Tonight he was actually looking forward to the event because he'd sent a note to Ally's room earlier with an invitation for her to join him. There was nothing personal about it. It wasn't as if she'd be the only one there. There would be six others, not counting himself, and a good reason for her not to eat alone. If she was as troubled as he'd been when he came, he knew she would need to focus on something besides herself. And there was no better way to achieve that than to sit at a dinner table with six perfect strangers—seven counting him—and remember that there was a world outside the realm of SPEAR.

He told himself he was just doing his job. And he believed it, all the way to the dining room and right up to the point when Ally entered the room.

It was the traditional, little black dress—simple in style, skimpy in fabric—and on Ally Corbin, pure dynamite. East knew he was staring, but he couldn't seem to stop. It wasn't as if he never saw beautiful women, because he did—daily. And it wasn't as if he didn't have opportunities to enjoy their company. It was that he usually chose not to. But this time it was different. There was an urgency within him to connect with her on something other than this ephemeral, holiday basis. He kept thinking that if he let her leave without pursuing this desire, he would regret it for the rest of his life.

Then he shoved back the thought and stood, smiling cordially as he pulled out a chair and seated her. He needed his head examined. She was here to recuperate. Period.

He touched her shoulder briefly. "I'm so glad you felt like joining us. The food is particularly exceptional tonight." Then he added with a wink. "I know because I stole a couple of bites when the chef wasn't looking."

Everyone at the table laughed along with Ally as East took his seat at the head of the table.

"Thank you for inviting me," she said, and pretended that her heart was not in her mouth as she gave him a surreptitious glance.

Mercy, but that man certainly knew how to fill out a dinner jacket and slacks. She'd heard of clothes making the man, but in this case, it was just the opposite. There was barely time for her to be introduced to the others before a waiter appeared to take their orders.

And so the evening began.

Ally sat through one course after another, smiling and nodding and offering small bits of herself into the conversation. But her heart wasn't in it. Every time she looked at East, she fought rising panic. How could she possibly broach the subject of her mission without angering him? What could she say to convince him to go back on active duty that Jonah hadn't already said? She watched the way his mouth tilted and curved as a smile tugged at his lips and the way his eyes glittered when something moved him to a passionate response. Every time he reached for his wineglass, she caught herself staring at the way his massive hand would curl so delicately around the fragile stem.

She glanced down at the napkin she'd wadded in her lap and sighed. Never in her life had she felt so inadequate. She sighed again and looked up, only to find herself pinned under the dark, watchful stare of her host. Heat rose up her neck to her cheeks, spreading across her face like water lapping against the shore. Good Lord. She was blushing and he could see. If he grinned, she was going to have to hate him, and that thought alone made her mad.

To her relief, he was the first to look away. Soon afterward, Ally made her excuses and left, fully intent on going back to her room. She never made it past the lobby.

"Ms. Corbin...Ally...wait!"

She pivoted sharply, surprised that he'd followed her.

"Are you all right?"

The gentleness in his voice was almost her undoing. He was being so kind and when he found out why she was here, it would ruin everything. Then her shoulders slumped. Ruin everything? What was the matter with her? There wasn't anything to ruin.

"I'm fine," she said. "Just tired."

East hesitated, for some reason, still reluctant to let her go. "Would you like to take a walk? Maybe some fresh air would do you good."

Her heart skipped a beat. The perfect opportunity to establish a little one-on-one rapport. For business reasons of course.

"Yes, I believe I would," she said. "Should I get a sweater?"

His gaze raked her bare, slender arms and then up the length of her neck, to her mouth, before he made himself focus.

"If you get cold, you can use my jacket."

"You've been far too kind already. All this personal service is going to go to my head and now you're offering your jacket? Are we still on a no-tip basis?"

He grinned. Damned if he didn't like her attitude as much as that dress she was wearing.

"Something tells me it would be hard to feed you a line," East said. "To use one of my grandfather's favorite phrases, you're a saucy little thing, aren't you?"

She frowned. "I don't know. I certainly never thought of myself as saucy. My parents always said I was forthright. Alicia is a forthright child. Not funny. Not pretty. Not even cute. Just forthright." She smiled, unaware of the poignancy in her voice. "What does it take to be saucy?"

At that moment, she reminded him of his son, Jeff. At least the way Jeff had been when they met. A little wary of East and a whole lot unsure of himself. His heart went out to her then, in a way it might never have done, otherwise.

"I don't exactly know," he said gently. "Maybe a little extra gumption and a whole lot of guts."

Suddenly, the conversation had gotten too personal for Ally and she didn't know where to go with it. Teasing with the opposite sex in any form, whether it was flirtatious or sexual, was not something she could do.

She glanced toward the door. "About that walk?"

He took off his coat and draped it around her shoulders.

The warmth of his body was still on the fabric as it wrapped around her. She swallowed nervously. "I didn't say I was cold."

"Good. Now you won't have to," he said shortly, and took her by the elbow and led her out into the night.

Chapter 3

Despite the well-lit grounds surrounding the hotel, East headed directly for the shadows, taking Ally with him. In a way, she understood his need to walk in darkness. In their business, anonymity was often the difference between life and death, and even though East no longer put his life on the line on a daily basis, old habits obviously died hard.

"Is this the way to the beach?"

He stopped and turned, a shadowy silhouette against the night.

"No. Would you rather go down to the beach?"

She started to deny his question, then convinced herself that truth, at least as far as she could take it, would probably work better between them.

"Yes, actually I would, if it's not too much trouble?"

From the tone of his voice, she thought he smiled.

"Trouble? To walk on a beach in the moonlight with a beautiful woman? Ms. Corbin, you crush my ego."

Ally stifled a snort of disbelief. "I'm sorry, Mr. Kirby, but your reputation precedes you. From what I've been told, both your ego and reputation are indestructible."

When he answered, the smile was gone from his voice.

"If only that were so," he said, then took her by the arm. "Allow me. The steps are lit, but uneven. And when we get to the beach, I'm afraid those shoes you're wearing will be more of a hindrance than help."

Thankful for the cover of darkness, Ally rolled her eyes at her own stupidity. She'd royally botched her first opportunity to do what she'd come to do. She was supposed to talk him into returning to work for Jonah, not remind him of why he quit in the first place. When his fingers curled around the flesh of her upper arm, she swallowed nervously, picturing the way they'd looked curling around that fragile stem on his wineglass. Long. Strong. Deadly.

As they descended the well-lit steps to the beach below, the silence between them was awkward, but when they reached the sand and Ally bent down to take off her shoes, something changed. Maybe it was the sound of rolling surf, or the path of moonlight stretching upon the water. And maybe, it was just the fact that in that moment, Ally quit thinking about why she'd come and began to focus on where she was. She turned, staring in awe at the luminous majesty before her.

"How beautiful."

"Yes…beautiful," East said.

Ally was so caught up in the view, she didn't realize that he was staring at her and not the moon.

Time passed. The moon climbed higher in the night sky and the wind rose with it. A sense of sadness came upon her, knowing that this night and the spell of it all would never come again in quite the same way. Impulsively, she took a step toward the ocean, but East's grip on her arm tightened, and he held her back.

"It's too cold," he said softly.

She started to argue. All she'd wanted was to feel the pull of the ocean against her feet to see if it matched the rhythm of her heart, and then she realized that coddling a flight of fancy was not why she'd come. And, since she'd already broken the tenuous connection they'd made with her thoughtless remark earlier, she felt obliged to call it a night.

"Of course, you're right. I don't know what I was thinking. It's late and I'm sure you have more important things to do than baby-sit me." She handed him his sports coat. "Thank you for the loan. I think I'll go to bed now."

East found himself holding his jacket as Ally bolted toward the steps leading back to the hotel.

"Well, hell," East muttered, then followed her ascent, but by the time he entered the lobby, she was nowhere in sight.

East's sleepless night was exacerbated by the turmoil to which he awoke the next morning. Both a knock on his door and the frantic ringing of both his cell phone and telephone had him on his feet and grabbing for a pair of sweats before he'd barely opened his eyes. He grabbed the cell phone on the way to the door, growling a response into the receiver as he unlocked the door.

The chef was on the cell phone yelling in his ear as

Foster Martin, the assistant manager, dashed inside his apartment with a separate, but equally frustrating problem. He clenched his jaw, motioning for Foster to sit as he turned his attention to the man on his cell phone.

"Please hold a moment, my other phone is ringing."

He answered the phone on the table without showing his frustration.

"This is Kirby."

"Mr. Kirby, this is Detweiler."

East flinched. The only time his head of security called was when there was a problem.

"What's up?" he asked.

"There's a woman giving birth in Room two, one, five."

East groaned. The last time this happened, the woman filed a lawsuit against them for not having a doctor on staff. She didn't win, but it was a hassle that lasted the better part of six months. He didn't want a repeat performance.

"You've called 9-1-1?"

"They're on the way."

"How far along is she?"

Detweiler began to stutter. "Far along? Hell if I know. She's at the screaming stage, if that's what you want to know."

East almost chuckled. If he remembered correctly, Detweiler was a bachelor.

"I don't suppose there's a doctor registered?" East asked.

Foster jumped up from where he'd been sitting, waving his hands even more in an attempt to get East's attention.

"There is, there is," Foster cried. "His name is

Butcher. I remember thinking that would be a terrible name for a doctor to have.''

East gave Foster a nod and then returned to his conversation with his security chief.

''Check with registration. There's a Doctor Butcher staying here. Get him to the woman's room asap. I'll be there as soon as I can.''

''He's in three hundred,'' Foster said. ''I checked him in myself yesterday.''

''Did you hear that?'' East asked.

''Yeah, Room three hundred,'' Detweiler said, and hung up.

Foster started to speak when East motioned to the cell phone he was still holding.

''Hello, Pete, you still there?'' East asked.

A soft curse rolled across East's eardrum, followed by a burst of anger. ''Pierre, Pierre, I told you to call me Pierre. And I do not like to be kept waiting.''

East's voice lowered. ''Look Fullbright, pull that French stuff with someone who hasn't known you since sixth grade, okay?''

Pete Fullbright cursed once more, with emphasis, then sighed.

''The entire meat shipment is bad. What the hell do you suggest we serve three hundred and forty-four guests today? Hmmm?''

''Call Antonelli's Meat Market. It's just a twenty minute drive from here as opposed to the two-hour trip from L.A. Have them deliver whatever they have that's freshest, and to hell with the cost. We'll take it out of our regular shipper's hide later.''

''Bien, bien,'' Pete said. *''Merci.''*

East grinned. ''Hey, Pete, you need to practice that

accent a little more. It still sounds like you're saying *mercy*.''

''Go to hell,'' Pete muttered, then added, ''...boss. Go to hell, boss.''

''Been there, done that,'' East said, and disconnected, turning his attention to the man on his couch. ''Now, what's up with you?''

Foster Martin stood abruptly, his hands fluttering about his chest like a wounded bird trying to find the strength to land.

''The computer is down. At least I think it's down. Anyway, it won't come up and we have guests waiting to check out and guests waiting to check in. I've already called our usual repair service and they're on some emergency call on the other side of L.A. Said it would be this afternoon before they can get out here.''

''Then call someone else,'' East said, and headed for the kitchenette. Before any other disaster presented itself, he needed fortification in the form of caffeine.

''But...''

East pivoted, staring sharply at the small, pale man and tried to remind himself why he'd ever hired him. Then he frowned, remembering. He was the Attorney General's nephew and he hadn't hired him. He'd just appeared one day with a letter of recommendation written on a letterhead he couldn't ignore.

''Foster, is there a phone book in your desk?''

''Why...yes there is. Do you want to borrow it?'' Foster asked, anxious to please.

East bit his lip to keep from shouting. ''No, but I want you to use it. Find the yellow pages. Find someone who can work on our specific system, and get them out here, okay?''

"Yes…yes, okay," Foster said, and bolted toward the door.

"Oh, and Foster…"

He stopped and spun, his hands still fluttering. "Yes?"

"About the guests wanting to check in or out, use a pen and paper and do it like we used to before computers were ever invented."

"Yes. All right," he said, and shut the door behind him.

The ensuing silence lasted long enough for East to get his coffee made. As it was perking, he quickly dressed and made a trip to Room two hundred and fifteen to check on the expectant mother. To his relief, he found Doctor Butcher in the act of delivery and a couple of paramedics on their way down the hall, although the young woman was wailing at the top of her voice because her husband was nowhere in sight. It seems he'd gone out for his morning jog and was missing the birth of their first child. At that point, East made a quick call downstairs to send a couple of staffers in search of the man. Once he was certain that everything was under control, he dashed back to his room. After a couple of cups of coffee and a shower and shave, he headed downstairs fully expecting to find chaos at the registration desk. Instead, the desk was almost empty and only the normal ebb and flow of traffic was moving through the lobby. Mildly surprised, he moved behind the counter then into the staff room where the mainframe computer was housed.

Ally looked up from the chair in which she was sitting. "Good morning," she said, then returned her attention to the computer terminal in front of her.

East's mouth dropped. "This area is off-limits to the

guests," he said, then remembered who he was talking to and changed the direction of his questions. "What are you doing?"

Her fingers paused on the keys and the look she gave him was just shy of a smirk.

"I think my security clearance is high enough that I can be trusted," she drawled, then tapped a couple more keys, hit the Save button, and leaned back in her chair with a satisfied smile. "There, that should do it."

"Do what?" East said, moving to look over her shoulder.

She stood. "Keep your system up and running for a few more years."

"You fixed it?"

She nodded as she moved toward the door. "I'm going to get some breakfast now. That's where I was going when I saw all the commotion. I offered to help and your assistant, what's his name…?"

"Foster. Foster Martin."

"Oh yes, Foster." She grinned. "He's not exactly cool under fire, is he?"

East sighed. "Was spit dribbling from the corners of his mouth?"

Her grin widened. "Only the left one."

"Great," East muttered, then shoved a hand through his hair in frustration. He glanced at the computer, which seemed to be running normally. "What did you do to it?"

Her smile stilled and she shrugged. "Oh…just dug around a little on the hard drive, punched in a few commands and gave it a new lease on life, so to speak."

"That's impossible. There are passwords."

She folded her hands in front of her like a child about to recite.

"No, it's not impossible and yes, I know."

He arched an eyebrow. "So your line of expertise for SPEAR is in computers?"

Ally shook her head. "Not really. They use me mostly for undercover work. Without makeup, I can pass for a teenager pretty easy."

"Computers are a hobby then?"

The smile on her face kept getting smaller. "No, I just know stuff," she said, and once again started toward the door. She wanted to get out before he got to the part where he found out that her IQ was bigger than his ego. It always turned men off and she didn't want to see that happen again. Not now. Not with him.

But East wasn't going to let go. He caught her by the elbow as she started to pass.

"Stuff? You call that stuff? It took three technicians two days to set up this system. It's complicated as hell and linked to Monarch's entire chain of resorts and you not only got into the system, but had it up and running within thirty minutes?"

Ally stopped, her chin lifting as she met his gaze.

"Actually it was about ten. I know things. Lots of things, okay? Can we leave it at that?" Then she quietly pulled away from his grasp.

East hadn't realized he was still touching her and took a quick step back, aware that he'd invaded her space and even more aware that she didn't like it.

"I'm sorry," he said. "I didn't mean to be..." He sighed and started over. "Look, I guess what I should be saying is thank you."

"You're welcome."

She was all the way to the door when his voice stopped her.

"Ally."

She bit her lip, then turned. "Yes?"

"Intelligence isn't something to be ashamed of."

"Intelligence is hardly the word society uses to describe someone like me," she said, unaware of the anger in her voice.

East moved toward her, touching her shoulder, then dropping his hand. His voice was soft, his gaze compelling. She found herself unable to look away.

"Exactly what *do* they call someone like you, then?"

"Freak of nature was the favorite phrase at my alma mater."

"How old were you when you graduated?"

Her gaze turned inward, remembering how ill-equipped she'd been at ten years old to handle the social aspect of higher education.

"From high school…ten. From college…seventeen. But that was with three Ph.D.s and a minor in foreign languages, six to be exact. I was considering another semester or two when SPEAR recruited me. The rest is history."

East kept looking at her, trying to imagine what it would be like to live with so much knowledge and not go crazy at the rest of the world's ineptitude. He gave her a long, cursory stare.

"So, what you're saying is, if I asked real nice, you could do my taxes for me next year without breaking a sweat?"

Her eyes narrowed as she stared hard at his face. "Are you teasing me?"

"Yes."

"Oh." She managed a smile.

He pointed toward the door with his chin. "Still hungry?"

Her stomach grumbled. "Starving."

"Then follow me. I've got an in with the cook. He makes the best waffles this side of St. Louis."

"Who's in St. Louis?" she asked as they headed out the door.

"Aunt Dinah. Hers are the best, but don't tell Pete I said so."

"Who's Pete?"

"My fake French chef," East said. "Do you like them with whipped cream and strawberries, or are you a syrup fan?"

"Actually, I favor peanut butter and grape jelly."

East grinned. "Order it on the side or Pete will have himself a fit."

She pursed her lips primly. "Pete needs to learn to savor the finer things in life."

East laughed aloud.

As they exited the office, a frantic young man in jogging clothes came running through the lobby. He took one look at East and started yelling.

"My wife. My wife. They said she was in labor."

This would be the missing father, East thought, and took him by the shoulders, fixing him with a calm, steady gaze.

"Take it easy, Dad. She's fine. There's a doctor and a couple of paramedics with her now."

The expression on the man's face went from shock to joy.

"Dad?"

"I think I heard them say it was a boy," East said.

"Oh man, oh man. I'm a father. I'm a father," he cried.

"Yeah, so am I," East said. "Congratulations."

The man bolted for the stairs, unwilling to wait for an elevator.

East was still smiling when he turned back to Ally.

"Sorry. It isn't usually so hectic around here."

"Compared to my job, this is nothing," Ally said.

The look on her face made him hurt. He remembered all too well what that job could be like, but before he could comment, his cell phone rang again. Within moments of answering, he began to frown.

"Hang on a minute, please," he told his caller, then touched Ally's arm apologetically. "I'm sorry. I have to take this call. Why don't you head for the terrace. There's a buffet set up, or you can order for both of us. Either way, I'll be there shortly."

"Sure, but what do you want?"

"Just tell the waiter I'll have my usual." Then he added. "Don't wait on me. I wouldn't want those waffles to get cold."

"Actually, they're better that way."

He shook his head and then chuckled. "Do you have any other *interesting* habits I should know of?"

"I don't know," Ally said. "Exactly what do you think you should know about me?"

East's smile slipped as his eyes suddenly darkened. "I'm not sure, are you?"

Suddenly, his question took on a whole other meaning. She looked away, and then angry with herself for being so gutless around this man, made herself look at him.

"Around you, I'm not sure of anything." Then she doubled up her fists and thumped the sides of her legs in frustration. ''And, I don't think I was supposed to tell you something like that. Damn it all to hell, I am not good at this stuff.''

She stomped away, leaving East to make of her outburst what he would. Then he remembered his caller and put the phone back to his ear.

Ally sat on the terrace with her chin in her hands, staring out at the Pacific. This whole thing was a fiasco. Jonah must have been desperate to even consider someone like her for this task. She kept wanting to blurt out the reason she was here and get it over with. Subterfuge was a part of her life, but she'd never used it on one of the ''good guys.'' Deceiving East didn't feel right and the longer she played the part of a stressed-out operative, the closer it came to being the truth. If she told him now, the worst that could happen was he'd just tell her to get lost. Then all she had to do was tell Jonah she failed.

She sighed.

Therein lay part of her problem. In all of Ally's life, she'd never failed at anything, except maybe relationships.

Her eyes narrowed thoughtfully as she continued to watch the breakers slamming against the rocks. There had to be a way to accomplish this.

A few moments later, a waiter brought her food, with the comment that he would serve East's order when he arrived.

Ally nodded.

''Will there be anything else?'' he asked.

''Not right now,'' she said. ''Thanks.''

She reached for the side dish of peanut butter as he walked away and began carefully smearing each square in her waffle with an equal amount of the rich, creamy spread. Once having achieved symmetry, she did the same with the grape jelly until the waffle was all but obliterated beneath the concoction. Then, with a knife and fork, she cut into the waffle, separating a perfect three-square by three-square bite and popped it into her mouth. Her eyes rolled with appreciation as she began to chew.

East stood in the doorway leading out to the terrace, stealing a moment to watch Ally unobserved. At first glance, there wasn't anything really remarkable about her. She was of average height, without an ounce of spare flesh on her body. Her clothes were ordinary; a pair of navy slacks and a white, linen shirt hanging loose about her hips. Her hair was short and capped her head in a thicket of auburn curls and her eyes were the color of new grass. And yet as he watched her methodically preparing her food, he understood her need for control.

He could only imagine what it must have been like for a child such as she; born with an intelligence beyond understanding into a family that didn't have time for her, she must have felt like a misfit from the beginning. He didn't know, but he would guess she'd never had a "best friend" in her life and wondered if, as a child, she'd ever spent the night giggling with other girls or playing with dolls. Being a SPEAR operative wasn't conducive to gathering close friends, either. Too many secrets that couldn't be shared.

When she slowly and carefully cut another perfect square of waffle and popped it into her mouth, he was struck by an overwhelming urge to lean over her shoulder and take a great big bite out of the middle of that waffle just to see what she'd do when things went out of control.

At that moment, her waiter stopped at her table and topped off her coffee. When she lifted her head to smile and thank him, East pictured himself leaning down and tasting the peanut butter and jelly waffle on her lips. In spite of how physically resilient he knew she must be, there was something very fragile about her insecure smile and the curve of her cheek.

But he'd been too accustomed to denying himself to do anything so foolish as to get involved with a woman—especially an operative. After what he'd done, he didn't deserve happiness. It was enough that he was still alive. The kid he'd hit with his car was not.

He shoved aside his personal feelings as he strode to their table and took his seat. "Looks good," he said, pointing toward the food on her plate as the waiter filled his cup.

"Umm," she nodded, still chewing.

"Your food is ready, sir," the waiter said. "I'll be right back with it."

"Good, I'm starved," East said, taking a careful sip of the hot brew in his cup.

Suddenly, Ally gasped as a seagull swooped into their line of vision, filched a piece of left-over toast from a nearby table that had yet to be bussed and then disappeared over the roof of the hotel.

"They're pests, but this is their territory and there's little we can do about them if we choose to eat outdoors."

"I rather like them," Ally said. "I just wasn't expecting it, that's all."

East watched her pick up her knife and start to cut

through her food, again sectioning off that same three-by-three square bite. Her forehead was knotted in serious concentration and she was gripping her knife and fork so hard that her knuckles were almost white. He frowned, believing that she was closer to a breakdown than he first suspected. Instinctively, his need to help her kicked in and he leaned forward.

"Why do you do that?"

She paused and looked up. "Do what?"

He pointed to the waffle. "Cut your food so precisely."

Startled, she glanced down at her plate then felt herself flushing with embarrassment. Freak. Always a freak.

"I don't know," she said. "I suppose it's just a habit." She laid down the knife and fork and then folded her hands in her lap, her enjoyment of her food suddenly gone.

"Ah, damn, I didn't mean to upset you," East muttered.

Ally made herself smile. "Don't be silly. I don't get upset."

That cold, emotionless wall had gone up between them again and East found himself resenting its presence. By God, he was going to get an emotional response from her, even if it was nothing but anger.

"Yes, you do. Everyone does at one time or another."

Ally bristled. She hadn't known this man even twenty-four hours and he thought he "knew" what she was thinking?

"Listen, Mr. Kirby, you don't know me, so how can you sit there and pretend you know my behavior patterns?"

The flush on her face had gone straight to her cheeks. They were fiery with anger, matching the glitter in her eyes. East leaned back in his chair, satisfied with what he'd done. She didn't know it yet, but she would thank him one day for putting her mind on something besides the hell that had driven her here.

"You gonna eat that?" he asked, pointing to the leftover food on her plate.

Prepared for another stinging rebuttal, his question took her off guard. "Umm...I, uh...don't suppose."

"Good," he said, and pulled the plate in front of him, then picked up the waffle like a piece of toast and took a hearty bite. As he chewed, his eyebrows arched in surprised appreciation. Then he swallowed. "Not bad," he said. "Not bad, at all," and opened his mouth again.

Suddenly, Ally regained her sense of self and snatched the waffle out of his hands just in time to save it from another bite.

"I changed my mind," she said. "You eat what you ordered and I'll eat mine."

Ally stared down at her plate and the chaos he'd made of the waffle. Sighing, she reached for her fork when she heard him clear his throat. She looked up, glaring at the smug expression on his face. *Damn him. There's nothing wrong with being a little bit fussy about one's food.*

"What?" she asked.

He shrugged, as if to say he didn't know what she was asking.

"That's what I thought," she snapped. As she began trimming off the uneven spot he'd bitten into, she heard him chuckle.

"Just because I don't want to share my food, doesn't mean there's anything wrong with me," she muttered.

East's grin stilled. He leaned forward. "Ally."

"What?" she mumbled, refusing to look up.

"I was just teasing you. There isn't a damn thing wrong with you, do you hear me?"

She paused, letting an old pain resettle itself around the region of her heart. Then, just to prove she was as outrageous as the next, she set her jaw and cut a reckless swath through the chilling waffle, slashing off a diamond-shaped bite, rather than her usual, perfect square. Then she gave him a "take that" look and stuffed the bite into her mouth just as their waiter appeared with East's breakfast.

East hid a grin as the waiter set down his food. Moments later, he dug into his scrambled eggs and bacon. As he ate, he couldn't help thinking they'd never tasted so good and wondered if it was the waffle appetizer that had piqued his appetite, or the company he was in. Either way, for a day that had started off so chaotically, it was turning into something very interesting.

Chapter 4

Rain drifted in blowing sheets, hammering against the windows of the two-story cabin overlooking the gorge below. Normally the view was magnificent and the isolation well suited to Jonah's needs, but not today. The only way off the mountain was by helicopter or on foot, and until the storm passed, neither was possible.

He paced the floor between windows and walls, his anger growing at the latest news he'd just received. A courier had just been arrested at the Iranian border carrying highly classified documents. Documents that led straight back to him. And if that wasn't damning enough, there was the matter of one-hundred thousand dollars recently deposited into his personal bank account that he could not explain.

"Damn, damn, damn it to hell," Jonah growled, then pivoted sharply and slammed his fist into a wall.

If it wasn't for the President's intervention, the Attorney General would already be issuing a warrant for his arrest. He didn't know how much longer he could fend off these assaults on his credibility and character. Immediately his thoughts went to Alicia Corbin. Before, he'd been willing to give her plenty of time to play on Easton Kirby's guilt, but this latest stunt with the foreign courier changed everything. Whoever was trying to ruin him was escalating the incidents. Time was no longer on his side. She'd been there almost a week and he needed to know what was happening at Condor Mountain Resort, because if East couldn't be persuaded to help, he was going to be forced to look to someone else. But to whom? The only reason he'd approached East in the first place was because he didn't know who else to trust.

A muscle jerked at the side of his jaw as he strode toward the fireplace. With a quick twist of his wrist, he turned the iron lion's head finial on the corner of the mantel. Immediately, a portion of the paneling slid into a pocket in the wall, revealing its secrets—the main communication center for SPEAR. He wasn't the first Jonah to occupy this place and he wouldn't be the last, but if he didn't resolve this mess and soon, his tenure would soon be over.

In the corner, a state-of-the-art fax hummed silently as page after page was fed into a tray, while line after line of text scrolling on a nearby computer terminal was saved for later review. Every up-to-date communication option known to man was there before him and yet with all of it at his fingertips, he still couldn't find the one man intent on ruining his life.

A flat map of the world hung at eye level from the ceiling, imprinted on a large sheet of clear Plexiglas. The series of black intersecting marks were the locations of ongoing, world-wide investigations by SPEAR, but it was the red markings with which he was most concerned. They were the ones that pinpointed him as being involved in a subversive activity. He picked up a red dry-marker from the tray below and circled the border crossing where the courier had just been arrested, then stepped back to study the pattern. But the longer he stared, the more certain he was that there was no pattern, only a series of random incidents targeted for one purpose—to bring him down. At that point, a calm came over him. By God, he hadn't survived this long only to be brought down like this.

He moved toward his desk with purpose, then dropped into his chair, leaning forward and staring intently at the bank of phones within arm's reach. But it was the red phone on which he was focused. Within seconds, his mind had skipped through a half-dozen scenarios and chosen one best suited for this task. Without hesitation, he lifted the receiver to his ear. Two hours later, a package for Alicia Corbin was delivered to the front desk of Condor Mountain Resort.

The phone in East's office rang just as he was entering the last set of figures for his quarterly report. Grateful for the interruption, he hit the Save button on the computer keyboard and reached for the phone.

"Hello."

"Hey, Dad, it's me."

The familiar growl of Jeff's voice made him smile.

"Hey, yourself, stranger. When are you coming home for a visit?"

Jeff snorted with disbelief. "With my schedule, you've got to be kidding, right? The better question is, when are you coming to see me?"

East stood abruptly, shouldering the wave of instant guilt. "It has been a while, hasn't it, son?"

"Almost two months."

"And, so you're trying to tell me that you feel abandoned? What happened to that girlfriend you didn't want to discuss? Is she history?"

There was a brief silence, then Jeff laughed, but East thought it sounded forced.

"No, I'm not feeling abandoned. I'm just tired, and heartily sick of my own cooking. And I'm not in the mood to discuss women, period."

East chuckled. "That bad, huh?"

"Yes."

"So, let's talk about something simple then, like maybe your classes or your rotation at the hospital. Which one are you on now?"

Jeff laughed. Calling what he did "simple" was a joke and East knew it. "Pediatrics. And I'm ready for that to be over," he said, and then sighed. "Which is not to say I don't like kids, because I do, but there's something about kids and incurable illnesses that I can't get past."

East remained silent, sensing that Jeff just needed to talk, which he continued to do.

"Dad, there's this seven-year-old kid named Darcy. She's got ten of the cutest little brown freckles across her nose and the biggest blue eyes I've ever seen and she asked me yesterday if I'd marry her when she grows up." His voice broke. "Damn it, Dad, she's missing her two front teeth and all of her hair and she's dying, and there's not a goddamned thing anyone can do for her."

"I'm sorry," East said quietly. "That's got to be tough."

Jeff took a slow, shaky breath. "Sorry, it's just that sometimes this stuff gets to me…you know?"

Images flashed through East's mind—flashes of gunfire, blood splatters on his shoes from the agent who'd just died at his feet, days and nights spent in swamps with nowhere to sleep.

"Yeah, I know."

He stood abruptly and turned to the bank of windows behind his desk, staring absently through the glass without actually seeing the idyllic view of the beach below.

"Look, if you'll give me a few days to clear my calendar and make sure that my assistant can cover for me, I'll make a run to L.A. Just fax me your schedule so I won't interfere with your work or classes."

"Fantastic! I'll get the info to you sometime within the next day or two." The tone of his voice lifted. "I can already taste that steak."

East laughed. "Hungry for beef, are you? What have you been eating?"

"My cooking and everybody else's leftovers at work."

East frowned. "Are you short of money, son?"

Jeff chuckled. "No, just time."

"You sure you want to waste it on me?" East asked.

"Spending time with you is never a waste."

The unexpectedness of Jeff's remark tightened the muscles in East's throat. "Thanks," East said. "Talk to you soon."

"Yeah, right," Jeff echoed. "Talk to you soon."

The click of the receiver, then the silence that came afterward was telling. Suddenly, the distance between East and his son seemed farther than ever. He hung up the phone and started toward the door when he paused, standing for a moment in the middle of the room and contemplating the solitude in which he lived. It seemed odd to consider that a man could be lonely while living among a constant stream of people, but it was true. In that moment, the longing for a personal connection, for someone to laugh with—someone to share troubles and joys and long, lonely nights with—was overwhelming.

The image of Ally Corbin's face moved through his mind, then he sighed as he walked out of his office to relieve Foster Martin. Even if he chose to pursue her, and even if she reciprocated his feelings, there were too many reasons why it would never work.

Ally breezed into the lobby, her arms full of packages. It was the seventh day of her stay at the hotel, but the first day she'd gone exploring since her arrival. Her hair was windblown and there was a small, brown stain on the knee of her white slacks from the chocolate ice-cream cone she'd been eating on the way home. But the light in her eyes and the smile on her face were too bright to notice such a small flaw. Somewhere between midnight and daylight last night she'd made a vow to herself that unless she began to act normal, East was going to suspect her motives for being here. And there was nothing more normal than a woman shopping. Thus the packages, thanks to the small arts and crafts community based at the foot of the mountain. And while she'd started out on the shopping spree as a cover, by the time she pulled into the parking lot of the hotel and began unloading her car, she realized how badly she'd needed the break. She hadn't done anything this ordinary in over a year and couldn't wait to get to her room and relive the joy of her new finds.

"Ms. Corbin! Ms. Corbin!"

She glanced toward the desk to the young man who was waving her down.

"Yes?"

"A package came for you while you were out."

Ally swerved toward him, laughing as she tried to juggle her load to allow for another item.

"I don't know where I'm going to put it, but…"

"Allow me."

She turned to find East behind her. Before she could argue, he'd relieved her of her bags, leaving her free to retrieve the package at the desk. Suddenly aware of how she must look, she nervously smoothed her hands down the front of her blouse and managed a smile.

"Well…uh…thank you. I'll just…"

"Take your time," East said.

The clerk handed her the small package and she quickly dropped it into her bag and dug out her room key. She gave East another nervous glance. He was waiting patiently.

"You don't need to bother—"

"It's no bother," East said. "Lead the way."

All the way to the elevator she kept resisting the urge to run a comb through her hair, then discarded the thought. *What I look like doesn't matter,* she scolded herself. *He's just being helpful. It's part of his job.*

When the elevator doors opened, she stepped inside then turned, giving him a quick, nervous smile as she inserted the key into the pad that would take the elevator straight to the penthouse.

East stifled a sigh. She'd looked like a windblown kid when she'd first entered the lobby, all pink-cheeked with flyaway hair. And that smudge on her pants. It looked like chocolate. She'd seemed so happy and now so ill at ease. Was it just him, or did all men evoke such a response from her?

"Looks like you've had quite a day," he said.

At his remark, her tension seemed to disappear.

"Oh, yes! It was wonderful. I found the most marvelous things. I can't wait to look at them all again."

He smiled. "That's good. Glad you found something enjoyable to occupy your time."

Her eyes lit up. "It was so much fun. I haven't done anything like this in ages. The only thing that could have made it better would have been sharing it with someone."

"If you'd asked, I would have been happy to—"

She blushed just as the door opened. "I wasn't fishing for an invitation," she said, and bolted into the small foyer leading to her door. With shaking hands, she punched in the security code and then opened the door and stepped aside, making room for him to enter.

"Just put them anywhere," she said. "And I really appreciate your help."

East dumped the bags on the sofa and then turned to look at her. She was still standing by the door, obviously waiting for him to leave. Despite the urge to linger, he could take a hint.

"See you at dinner tonight?" he asked.

"Yes. I'm starved already."

"Did you eat lunch?" he asked. "I can have something sent to your room."

"There's no need."

He frowned. "Have you had anything at all since breakfast?"

"Well, no, except an ice-cream cone. But I'm fine, really."

Still reluctant to leave, he glanced at the bags, curious as to what things would interest her.

"Find anything special?" he asked, pointing toward the bags.

For the first time since he'd relieved her of her bags, she gave him a genuine smile.

"Oh, yes! I collect music boxes and I found the most amazing one. It's not really a box, it's a snow globe, but it still plays music so I thought—"

"May I see?"

"Really? You really want to see?"

He nodded.

She slammed the door and bolted toward the sofa, then began digging through the bags.

As he watched, he remembered what she'd said about her parents' lack of interest in her childhood, and it occurred to him to wonder how many times in her life she had found pleasure, but had no one to share it with.

"Please, have a seat," Ally said. "It's going to take me a minute to find... No, wait, here it is."

She pulled a small box from a sack and then without thinking dropped onto the sofa next to where he'd sat down. She was so intent on unpacking the box that she didn't realize how intimate the moment had become; thighs touching, shoulders bumping as he leaned forward to see what she was digging out of the tissue.

She laughed to herself as she lifted it up, letting the light from a nearby window pierce the glass and highlight the figures within.

It was a miniature image of a cowboy on horseback with a small red and white calf lying across his lap and against the saddle horn. The cowboy was wearing blue jeans, a heavy sheepskin coat and a dark, wide-brimmed hat. He sat hunched in the saddle, leaning over the calf, as if sheltering it with his body. When she shook the globe, a sudden snowstorm appeared. Immediately, the viewer was drawn into the drama of the tender rescue of the calf from the storm.

"Isn't that the most amazing thing?" she said. Then she wound it up and tilted her head to one side, staring in fascination as the music began to play.

"What's that tune?" East asked.

She turned, her face alight with joy. "'Desperado'. It's an old Eagles song, but it fits, doesn't it?"

"Yes, it does," East said.

She looked back at the globe. "Isn't it pretty?"

"Very," he said softly, unable to take his eyes off her face.

Suddenly, aware of the brush of air against her cheek, she turned. Her eyes widened, her breath caught and then slowed. Long, endless seconds passed as they stared into each other's eyes, measuring the other's intent and the distance between their lips. The thought crossed her mind that if she leaned forward—

The music stopped.

Both of them blinked, as if startled to find themselves in such an intimate situation, but it was East who was the first to move away. Not because he wasn't tempted, because he was. But he kept remembering she was not only a guest, but had come here in a fragile condition.

"Sorry," he muttered. "I didn't mean to—"

Ally stood abruptly, the snow globe clutched to her chest like a shield.

"You didn't *do* anything, so an apology is uncalled for."

He followed her lead and got up as well. "Look, Ally, don't take me wrong. I—"

She lifted her chin and smiled. "Thank you for carrying my packages."

He fisted his hands, fighting the urge to shake that fake smile off her face.

"You're welcome," he said shortly. He walked to the door then turned, unwilling to leave her on such an uncomfortable note. "See you at dinner?"

"Of course," she said, and shut the door in his face.

"Well, hell," he muttered, and stomped toward the elevator.

"Damn, damn, damn," Ally moaned, and stomped toward the sofa, her joy in the snow globe forgotten.

It wasn't until she was changing her clothes that she remembered the package from the desk. Curious, she dug it out of her bag and began to unwrap it. But when a small black cell phone fell out of the packet with a note attached, her stomach knotted.

Jonah.

She picked up the note. As usual, Jonah's instructions were sparse and to the point.

Press the Send button. Let it ring twice then hang up.

She did as she was instructed, knowing that somewhere within the network of global communications, a chain of events was going off that would eventually alert Jonah that she'd received what he'd sent. Within a minute of her call, the small phone rang. With a sigh, she lifted it to her ear.

"This is Corbin."

The familiar rumble of Jonah's voice filled her ear.

"Are you well?"

"I'm fine, thank you. The weather here is marvelous.'' Then she frowned. He hadn't sent her here for a weather report. "I don't have much to tell you."

Jonah bit off an expletive. This wasn't what he wanted to hear, but it was hardly a situation he could force.

"What's the situation?"

She sighed and ran her fingers through her hair in a gesture of frustration.

"We've met, of course, even talked quite personally a couple of times. But he's not the most approachable person in the world and I'm not much good at employing feminine wiles."

Jonah almost smiled. She didn't know it, but that was exactly why he'd sent her. Easton Kirby was too shrewd a man by far to be swayed by something as sordid as impersonal sex.

"I didn't send you there to have sex with the man. You're the perfect woman for this job. You have a calm, rational approach to situations. Remember that and use it."

"Yes, sir," Ally muttered.

Jonah hesitated, but there was no need to delay the obvious.

"A situation has come up that has escalated the need for haste. Can you handle it?"

She swallowed nervously. "Yes, sir. I'll find a way. I won't let you down."

"Good. Oh, and keep the phone handy. It's programmed to contact me, and me alone. Do you understand?"

"Yes, sir."

"If it happens to fall into the wrong hands, it will self-destruct itself when used incorrectly."

"Right."

"I'm counting on you, Corbin."

"I won't let you down."

The line went dead.

Ally disconnected, too, then put the phone in her dresser, her joyous mood gone. She went back to the living room and picked up the snow globe, wound it up, then gave it a shake. Immediately, the snow and the music began to swirl around the lone cowboy and his mount. Her eyes narrowed as she stared, her thoughts in as much turmoil as the snow within the globe, and she didn't move until the music had stopped and the snow lay dormant in the bottom of the globe. Finally, she set it aside and started toward the bedroom to shower and change. East didn't know it yet, but tonight, he was going to get more on his plate than his dinner.

About a half-mile offshore, a lone yacht was dropping anchor for the evening while the staff began readying for the owner's evening meal. A man with a pair of powerful binoculars stood aft, ostensibly enjoying the view from the spacious white deck. But it wasn't the rhythmic rise and fall of seagulls over the water that captured his attention. His gaze was trained toward the beach and the hotel that sat on the rise above it. Even with the binoculars, he was unable to make out the faces of the people he saw, but he didn't care. He'd already confirmed that the people he sought were at the hotel, and it would only be a matter of time before he introduced himself—but in his own special way.

Despite the pep talk Ally had given herself while dressing for dinner, her stomach was in knots. It wasn't so much facing East that she dreaded, as the possibility of failing Jonah. She didn't know why the need for East to return to active duty was so important to Jonah, but she knew it must be vital for him to persist in such a fashion.

The dress she was wearing was simple, as were all of her clothes; it was of a white gauzy fabric with a scoop neck and loose, three-quarter length sleeves, and a hem that brushed the tops of her ankles as she walked. Her shoes were flat and little more than three straps; one across the back of her heel, the other two across the top of her foot. Her makeup was a reflection of how she saw herself—neat, coordinated and uncomplicated.

As she exited her suite and started down the elevator, she gave herself the once-over in the mirrored interior of the car. Satisfied that nothing was smudged or smeared and that her hair was in place, she lifted her chin and prepared to do battle. The car stopped once at the third floor. An elderly man and a young couple got on. The old man nodded at her, but the young couple had eyes only for each other. Ally tried not to stare, but their affection for each other was quite compelling and impossible to ignore.

It wasn't the first time in her life that she'd wished she'd been born an ordinary child and she let herself play with the idea of "what if" all the way down to the lobby. Yet when the doors opened and it was time to get out, reality returned. She wasn't ordinary and for some reason, she'd been entrusted with a job that was very important to Jonah. The fact that she'd never seen the man in her life did not negate the loyalty she felt for him. In an odd, even pitiful way, Jonah had become the father figure she'd never had. He asked things of

her that no one else would have even considered, but
always with the confidence that she would do a good
job, and when it was over, was forthcoming with his
praise. It didn't matter to her that she'd never felt his
arms around her or seen a smile on his face. It was all
about trust.

She strode into the lobby with that thought in her
heart, then noticed that she was a little earlier than the
time she'd planned to come down. A quick glance toward the terrace was all it took to draw her outside,
and as she took her place at the railing overlooking the
beach below, she realized she wasn't the only one
who'd had the same idea. The sun—in all its glory—
was about to set.

The water burned with a radiance, reflecting the colors hovering on the horizon, and the path of the sun
lay in a straight line upon the water, pointing toward
the beach below the hotel. If one was prone to fancy,
which of course Ally was not, one might have been
tempted to step onto that path, just in case it was as
firm as it appeared.

And that was how East found her, staring at the horizon with her elbows on the railing and her chin resting in her hands. The evening breeze was tugging at
the hem of her skirt, as well as the loose ends of her
hair, but she seemed oblivious to the taunt.

"Quite a view, isn't it?" he said softly.

Ally straightened abruptly and turned. "I didn't
know you were here."

His dark eyes bore down into her face, searching for
something. He didn't know what.

"Just arrived," he said, unwilling for her to know
that he'd been watching her for some time before his
approach. "Are you hungry?"

"Starved," she said, and was surprised to realize it was the truth. Suddenly, all her worries about facing this man faded in comparison to the beauty of what she'd just witnessed. "But before we go in, I have a question I need to ask you."

A little surprised, he hesitated, then nodded. "Of course. Ask away."

"Do you believe in repaying old debts?"

Immediately he thought of Jonah and his senses went on alert. But her face seemed so guileless, he chalked it up to guilt.

"Of course. I don't think a person can be free to go forward in life until old debts have been paid, whether monetary or emotional."

She nodded. "I agree," she said softly, then looked toward the dining room inside that was beginning to fill. "It's getting a little chilly out here. Shall we go inside?"

East offered his elbow and she accepted, as if taking the arm of a handsome man was an everyday occurrence for her. As he seated her, and then himself, it hit her how calm she was feeling, and moments later, knew why. The decision had been made and before the night was out, she would have stated her purpose and pled Jonah's case as eloquently as she possibly could. After that, it was out of her hands.

When East asked her what she wanted to eat, she laid her menu aside and blessed him with a rare smile.

"Order for me, too, will you? I'm in the mood to be surprised."

Chapter 5

Dinner was over and dessert had been ordered. The other two couples at their table had said their goodbyes and forgone the last course for a walk, instead. And although Ally wasn't really hungry for sweets, she held her ground, knowing that East would not abandon her to eat alone. It was the moment she'd been waiting for.

"The food was delicious," Ally said. "Thank you for such a fine meal."

East smiled. "Red snapper is a favorite of mine, especially when Pete serves it up Cajun by blackening the fillet as he did tonight."

She nodded, then glanced around, making sure that they were basically still isolated within the room. Satisfied that their conversation would not be overheard, she leaned forward, pinning East beneath the force of her gaze.

"Why did you refuse Jonah's request?"

East's smile froze, then disappeared. His fury was evident as his face suddenly paled.

"Son of a bitch."

Ally flinched inwardly, but she refused to let him know she was scared.

"He sent you, didn't he?"

"Yes."

It had to be said that East hadn't expected her honesty and it caught him off guard. He struggled with the need to throw something or throw her out of the hotel, but his anger landed somewhere between. He got up from the table and stalked off, leaving her behind.

It wasn't exactly the conversation Ally had hoped for, but nothing she hadn't expected. She caught up with him at the elevator and inserted herself between him and the wall.

"You didn't answer my question."

"Lady, I guarantee that right now you don't want to hear what I'm thinking, so why don't you take your little self off and mind someone else's business besides mine?"

The doors opened. Several guests got off. East got on and immediately pressed the Close Door button, unwilling to ride up with anyone else and have to deal with courtesies he wasn't feeling. But Ally was right behind him. To his dismay, he found himself enclosed in the small, mirrored car with her. Everywhere he looked, he saw a reflection of her face and the question in her eyes, still waiting to be answered.

"You told me you believed in paying back old debts. I didn't take you for a liar, Easton Kirby."

He spun, pinning her against the wall with the flat of one hand.

"You don't know what the hell you're talking about."

"I know that he saved your sanity and your butt by putting you in this job and that the one time he asked you for a favor, you refused him."

The doors opened and East pivoted, stalking off the elevator toward his personal quarters. Ally was still right behind him.

"Is that the way you repay Jonah, Mr. Kirby? For some reason known only to him, that man needs you and you've thrown up your hands and said no. Why? Because once upon a time someone died?"

He jammed his key in the lock and stormed inside. Before he could shut the door, she followed him inside.

"Shut up and get out!" he hissed. "You don't know what the hell you're talking about."

"I'll leave when I'm through," she snapped. "What I do know is that this is a war we're waging—a constant, daily war against crime and evil and all things ugly in this world and that sometimes in a war innocent people die. I know that. I've seen it firsthand, but it hasn't made me want to quit." Forgetting her earlier hesitation, she jabbed a finger against his chest. "What it has done is make me angry. And when I get angry, I want to get even. I want to take down the bad guys in a way that they will never come back. What I *don't* do is hide."

East inhaled sharply, stunned by her anger and her accusations.

"I didn't quit. I still work for SPEAR, just in another capacity. I fulfill a duty that might not be as dramatic as yours, but I am not hiding from the world."

She snorted beneath her breath. "You may have convinced yourself of that, but not me." Then she shoved her hands through her hair in frustration and started to pace. "Look, I don't mean to belittle your life. God knows it's true that you've already done your bit. You've already put yourself on the line more than most people, and what you're doing now is an important and honorable job." She stopped and turned, looking him straight in the face. "I don't know why Jonah needs you, but I suspect that you do, so can you look me in the face and tell me that whatever it is doesn't matter?"

A muscle jerked at the side of East's jaw. He knew it wasn't really her fault. She'd been following orders, just as he'd done many times before. But the thought did occur to him that for the first time in his life, he now understood what prompted the desire to kill the messenger for bringing bad news.

"Damn you," he muttered.

"No. You're damning yourself and I've done all I came here to do. The rest, Mr. Kirby, is up to you." She headed for the door.

"Where are you going?"

She stopped and turned. "To bed. Oh…and I imagine I'll be checking out sometime tomorrow so I'll tell you goodbye tonight. I can't say this trip turned out as I'd hoped, but I doubt I'll ever forget you."

Before he could answer, she'd slammed the door, leaving him with nothing but the echo of her words. With a heartfelt curse, he slumped into a nearby chair, leaned back and closed his eyes. It was going to be a hell of a long night.

It was six o'clock in the evening when Jeff Kirby unlocked the door to his apartment and then shouldered his way inside, dropping a backpack and an armful of dirty clothes on the floor by the door as he slammed it

Mission: Irresistible

shut behind him. Although the rooms were a bit dusty and there were some dirty dishes in the sink, he'd never been so glad to be home. He'd just finished a thirty-six hour stint at the UCLA Medical Center and was so exhausted he couldn't think. It had been all he could do to navigate the traffic from the hospital to his apartment. He headed for the bathroom, shedding his clothes as he went. All he wanted was a bath and a shower. He'd worry about the rest later.

When he stepped beneath the showerhead, he braced himself against the shower stall and bent his head, closing his eyes in silent ecstasy and letting the warm jets of water knead the knotted muscles in his neck and shoulders. He stood beneath the spray until he felt himself beginning to fold, then turned off the water and got out to dry. He could see the corner of his bed from where he was standing and kept picturing himself stretching out beneath the sheets.

With droplets still clinging to his back, he tossed his wet towel toward the rack as he walked past. It missed the hook and fell on the floor, but he kept on walking. When he reached the bed, he fell face forward upon the covers, his long bare legs and arms flung out. Within seconds, he was sound asleep.

The phone began to ring, but Jeff never moved. The sun set, the moon rose, and sometime after midnight he began to stir. His belly was empty and growling and his neck was stiff from the position in which he'd been lying. With a groan, he rolled over on his back and glanced at the digital clock on the table beside his bed.

It read 12:35 a.m. Already tomorrow. He had to be back at work in five hours. Alternating between the notion of going back to sleep and getting something to eat, his empty belly won out. He crawled out of bed and put on a pair of worn-out sweats on his way to the kitchen. Halfway down the hall he froze. Someone was rattling the knob on his front door.

His mind began to race. Had he turned the dead bolt when he came in, or in his exhaustion had he only turned the lock on the knob? He entered the living room just as the door to his apartment swung inward. Three men wearing dark coveralls and caps burst into the room.

He glanced toward the phone and when one of them yanked the jack from the wall, he realized they were already ahead of him. He doubled his fists.

They came at him from all directions, leaving him with nowhere to go but through them if he was to get out the door.

With a karate kick that his dad would have been proud of, Jeff connected with the first man, sending him flying backward with a kick to the chin. He hit the wall, taking down a table, a lamp and a picture as he fell. The noise was deafening. Jeff kept expecting that at any minute, Mil and Bill, his neighbors across the hall, would hear and come to see what was happening. While that man was scrambling to get up, the other two came at him on the run, hitting him squarely in the chest and taking him down beneath the weight of their bodies. More furniture crashed. Another lamp fell, shattering upon impact. Jeff landed one punch as the third man scrambled back up on his feet. After that, they had him subdued.

Blood ran freely from a cut inside his mouth and he could already feel his right eye swelling shut.

"If you sons of bitches planned on robbing me, you picked the wrong man. I don't have anything of value except a television, a VCR and about twenty dollars to

my name. Take the stuff and my car keys and just leave
me the hell alone.''

One of the men laughed. ''A smart-mouth. Boys, we
got ourselves a smart-mouth.''

He yanked Jeff to his feet while the other two began
wrapping duct tape around his hands and ankles. Jeff
continued to struggle, but it was useless. He thought of
his dad. What would he have done in such a situation?
Clues. That's it, clues. He would try to leave clues. But
what? My God, they hadn't exactly introduced themselves when they'd broken into his home.

As his mind was racing, one of the men bent over
and began wrapping his ankles. As he did, his shirt
sleeve slipped back, revealing an odd tattoo on his bi-
ceps. It was of an American Flag with the initials
B.O.B above it. It made no sense to him, but it was
the only anomaly he could see.

''The cops will be here any minute,'' he warned.
''My neighbors have probably already called them.''

The man looked up at Jeff and then laughed.

''Who? You mean those people across the hall? I
don't think so. About ten minutes ago they got a phone
call to come to UCLA Med Center and identify a body.
Damn shame about the woman's mother—her dying so
unexpectedly and all.''

Jeff's mind stopped. ''You killed an innocent
woman just to get rid of witnesses to killing me?''

''Hell, no. We're not killers, boy. We just gave them
a little fright. They're gonna find themselves the vic-
tims of a cruel joke. As for you, why, we're not going
to kill you, either. We're just gonna take you for a little
ride.'' Then he pointed toward the other two men.
''Straighten this place up. We wouldn't want anyone
to think he went against his will.''

''You bastard,'' Jeff snarled, and lowered his head, using it as a battering ram as he hit the man square in the belly.

They went down in a tangle of anger. Blood spurted inside Jeff's mouth upon impact, but it was nothing compared to the alarm in his heart. Unless a miracle occurred, he was about to be kidnapped, and he'd heard too many stories from his dad's past to believe that he would ever be rescued alive.

The man cursed and pushed, Jeff rolled, landing face down on the hardwood floor as the man put his boot in the middle of Jeff's back.

''Just stay put unless you want more of the same.''

Jeff groaned, but did as he'd been told. He watched from the corner as they began putting the apartment back in order, dumping broken glass in the wastebaskets and then carrying them into the hall and putting them down the garbage chute while the other one set the furniture back in place.

Suddenly, one of the men cursed and yanked off his glove.

''Cut my damned finger,'' he muttered, and wiped the blood on the seat of his pants, then dumped the last of the glass he was holding into a wastebasket.

Meanwhile, Jeff's thoughts were in turmoil. He had to leave some kind of clue, but what? His fingers were getting numb and he flexed them painfully. As he did, he felt moisture on the floor behind him and something clicked. Blood—his blood! He could use it like ink. But what to write? Again, his gaze fell upon the man with the odd tattoo and it clicked. Quickly, before they took him away, he traced the letters *B O B* on the floor with one finger. Within seconds, they were coming toward him.

"Get the trunk," the tattooed man said.

Afraid that they would see what he'd done, Jeff pretended to make one final escape by rolling away from the wall where he'd been lying. They laughed and caught him in the middle of the room.

"Where in blazes did you think you were goin', boy?"

Before Jeff could answer, he felt a prick on his arm then his ears began to buzz.

"What did you do?" he muttered.

"Come on, boy! Get up and get yourself in the trunk before you pass out on your face."

Jeff was fading fast. "Screw you," he said, as his eyes rolled back in his head.

"Damn it, Elmore, you could have waited until we got him in the trunk. Now we're gonna have to lift deadweight and me with a bad back."

"Just grab a leg and shut up," Elmore said. "The sooner we get back to Idaho, the better I'm gonna feel."

Somewhere between panic and pure nothing, Jeff registered what had been said, and then everything went black.

Morning came none too soon for Ally. She'd struggled all night with the urge to call Jonah and tell him she'd failed, but there was a part of her that still held out hope. The least she could do was give East until morning. If he hadn't changed his mind by the time she checked out, then would be soon enough to make the call.

Unwilling to see East again and face his bitterness and anger, she'd ordered breakfast sent up to her room, then wasted the biggest part of it, unable to eat for the pain. It was unusual for Ally to feel pain, because she had yet to suffer an injury in the field, and was rarely, if ever, ill. But the pain was there. Right around her heart. And every time she took a breath, it grabbed and tightened, squeezing until her eyes filled with tears. She kept seeing the look of disbelief on East's face turn from hurt and then to anger. She'd liked him—really liked him—and knowing she was the one who'd put this distance between them hurt even more.

With a dejected sigh, she dropped the last folded T-shirt into her bag and zipped it up, then put the cell phone Jonah had given her into her purse. It was her own fault. She'd known from the start that he wasn't going to appreciate being deceived. She grabbed a tissue from her pocket and gave her nose a quick blow. She just hadn't planned on being attracted to him. Intellectually, she knew that attraction between opposite sexes was nothing more than a secretion of pheromones. But intellect had nothing to do with her reaction to his deep, husky voice or the way his hands felt against her skin. And there was the way his eyes had turned dark when she thought he had been going to kiss her.

She dropped onto the side of the bed and covered her face with her hands. *Ah, damn. If only he'd kissed me. At least I would have had that to remember.*

The phone rang, startling her from her bout of pity. She grabbed it before it could ring a second time and then had to clear her throat of tears before she could speak.

"Hello?"

"Ms. Corbin, this is the front desk. We have a delivery for you. Shall we bring it to your room, or do you want to pick it up on your way out?"

Her heart skipped a beat. Could this be another package from Jonah? If it was, checking it out in the privacy of her room was better than in the front seat of a car.

"Bring it up, please. However, I'll be checking out soon."

"Yes, ma'am. Just let us know. We'll be happy to take care of your bags."

She set the phone back in the cradle and then went to the living room to await the delivery. A short while later, a knock sounded. She opened the door to find a bellhop holding a large manila envelope. She took it from him and then started to hand him some money when he waved it away.

"Oh no, ma'am. That's not necessary," he said, and shut the door behind him as he left.

"That's a first," she muttered, and put the money back in her pocket, then dropped the envelope on the table as if it were wired to explode before getting up the nerve to look inside. After a minute of deliberation, she dumped the contents upon the table. There were two items, a photo, which fell facedown, and a small white note card with a single phrase printed in heavy, black letters.

I know who you are.

Her heart skipped a beat. She picked up the photo and then inhaled sharply. Dear God. It was a picture of her and East standing out on the balcony last evening when they had watched the sunset.

She studied it for some time, trying to figure out what it was that bothered her, then it hit. Whoever had taken it, had done so from the water. They were being spied on, but why? It must have something to do with

Jonah. If it did, East would know. She turned toward the window overlooking the bay. But there was nothing in sight except whitecaps on the waves and a couple of sea lions sunning themselves on the rocks.

I know who you are.

She shuddered. The message was a warning. There was no mistaking that fact. And like it or not, she was going to have to confront East with this and then tell Jonah. She didn't relish doing either, but this note had just changed everything.

East had spent most of the night battling his conscience. On the one hand, everything Alicia Corbin had said to him was the truth. He did owe Jonah his sanity, maybe even his life. After the accident that had killed the kid, there had been many nights when he'd considered ending it all, telling himself that after what had happened, he didn't deserve to live, either.

But then he'd met Jeff, a fourteen-year-old runaway with no family, no roots, and no hope for a better life. Jeff had been street-smart and angry. Looking back, East knew that he'd subconsciously set out to save this kid because he hadn't been able to save the other one. But that was only at first. Within six months, his feelings for Jeff had truly changed. He cared about the boy who was trying to become a man on his own, and to his joy, Jeff was beginning to care for him. Somehow, Jonah found out and gave East the opportunity he needed to settle down by changing his status to inactive and putting him in charge of the Condor Mountain Resort. For the first time in his adult life, Easton Kirby had a permanent address and someone who depended on him, while Jeff gained a father and a home.

But that was ten years ago and East knew that if he died tomorrow, Jeff would survive. He was a big, savvy young man with a bright future ahead of him, and a good part of that was thanks to Jonah's intervention.

Now Jonah was calling in the marker and East had refused. The pressure was on and he didn't know where to turn. He'd been off active duty for so long, he felt as if technology and time had passed him by. There was so much about the business he didn't know anymore. It was frightening to think about holding Jonah's future in his hands. What if he failed? What if he made another mistake? This time, it would be Jonah who took the fall and the idea was impossible. The entire safety of the free world quite often fell on the shoulders of SPEAR operatives. Destroying Jonah could prove fatal to more than just the man, himself. It could affect the lives of every citizen of the United States of America, and thinking about the burden of responsibility made him sick. But the question kept coming back to the same answer. As Ally had reminded him quite forcefully, Jonah had asked. How could he possibly refuse?

It had taken all night and into the morning before East had gotten up the nerve to call Ally's room. But before he could act upon the thought, he'd gotten a call of his own—one that had taken him out of his own problems in a heartbeat. A child had gone missing.

East exited the elevator to find Foster Martin, the assistant manager, waiting for him. East acknowledged the man with an abrupt nod.

"What do we know?" East asked. "Have you searched the hotel? How old is he? Did you get a description of him, the clothes he was wearing?"

"I have staff searching every floor as we speak and the groundskeepers have just been alerted to search the surrounding area. The boy is almost three and wearing a pair of red swimming trunks. Nothing else."

"How do you lose a kid?" East muttered.

"Easy," Foster said. "All you have to do is blink."

East gave the man a considering look. "You sound as if you're speaking from experience."

"I lost my nephew while shopping last Christmas. I turned loose of his hand only long enough to get my wallet out of my pocket and when I reached down to get him, he was gone."

East sighed. At least he hadn't had that kind of problem with Jeff. He'd been past the hand-holding stage by the time that they'd met.

"I trust everything turned out okay?"

Foster nodded. "Thankfully, yes."

"Where had he gone?"

"Back to tell Santa to bring me a wife."

East grinned, then clapped Foster on the back. "It's too early for Santa, so let's go talk to the parents."

"They're outside right now with the bellhops who are searching the parking lot."

"Good. You stay inside and coordinate what you've already started. I'll go outside to see what I can do. Say a prayer."

"Yes, sir. Already done that, sir."

East started through the lobby, his focus on the situation at hand, and missed seeing Ally as she came off the elevator. But Ally saw him leaving and quickly followed, unaware of the unfolding drama. It wasn't until she'd exited the hotel that she realized something was amiss.

A young woman in hiking clothes came barreling around the corner of the building.

"Hey, what's going on?" Ally asked.

"Some little boy got himself lost. Everyone's helping search."

"What's he look like?" Ally asked.

The girl shrugged. "I don't know. All I heard them say is that he's little."

Ally sighed as the girl quickly left. First things first, and that meant finding the kid. But how? What would draw a child's attention in this place? There was no playground equipment, no swings, no playland via a fast-food restaurant. If he wasn't inside, then where would he be? She imagined the child being snatched, then blocked the thought out of her mind. Don't borrow trouble, she warned herself, and then took a deep breath and closed her eyes.

For a moment, all she could hear was the sound of voices calling back and forth as they searched, but she made herself block all that out and listen, instead, to the world around her.

The first thing she heard were the seagulls—the soft flapping of their wings as they rose and fell within the swells of the wind, and then their high-pitched calls. Goose bumps rose on the backs of her arms as she instinctively turned toward the sounds. She'd never really listened to the gulls before, but there was an eerie, almost otherworldly sound to their screech.

Then there was the rhythm of the waves, washing up, pulling back. A low, almost imperceptible sound came with it—a shrill, high-pitched shriek.

Her eyes flew open. Was that a gull? It came from

the back of the hotel, and there was nothing there but the steep, winding steps that led down to the beach. If the child was very small, surely he would not have been able to negotiate such an obstacle alone. Again, she heard a sound, only this time it didn't sound like a bird. It was the laughter of a child. She bolted toward the back of the hotel, hoping that she was wrong. And then she saw him and her heart stopped. She paused, then turned, shouting East's name.

Immediately, she saw East freeze and then turn. She shouted again, pointing toward the beach below, and then started to run. There was no time to waste on waiting for them to catch up, because the little boy was moving toward the water without realizing the terrible danger he was in. The first wave would knock him off his feet. The second one would pull him under. After that, it would be too late.

Chapter 6

Ally started down the steps, taking them two at a time and shouting as she ran, hoping to distract the little boy, but it did no good. He kept toddling toward the lip of the ocean, unaware of the danger, and she couldn't run fast enough to catch him. She was more than halfway down when East reached the top of the steps and started after her, but she didn't know it, and it would have made no difference if she had. She didn't even hear the child's mother suddenly scream out in horror, because the thunder of her own heartbeat was pounding in her ears. Her feet made hard, slapping sounds as she ran down the steps in a jarring rhythm, taking them two and three at a time. Once she slipped and, had it not been for the fierce hold she had on the handrail, would have gone head over heels down the rest. When she reached the last step, she came off of it in a leap, shedding her shoes and her shirt as she ran and leaving her in nothing but a bra and a pair of white cotton slacks.

''Noooo!'' she screamed, praying that the sound of her voice would stop the child in his tracks, but the word was lost in the shrieks of feeding gulls.

No more than fifty feet separated them when the first wave knocked the baby off his feet. He went down on his face, then came up crying. Ally saw the next wave coming and knew she was going to be too late. It rolled over him like a mother pulling a blanket over a sleeping child. There was a brief flash of red just below the surface of the water and then he was gone.

Precious seconds were wasted before Ally was in the water and running into the surf. Still focused on the last place she'd seen him, she took a deep breath and went headfirst into an oncoming wave, and then she, too, was gone.

A dozen frantic thoughts went through East's mind as he watched the water pull the baby under. But when Ally followed, too, then didn't come up, his heart nearly stopped. He was a good fifty yards behind her and time was not on their side. He knew within reason that she had to be an expert swimmer. All the SPEAR operatives were highly trained in all means of survival. But she didn't know this coast or its currents. There was a riptide about a hundred yards offshore and if she got caught in that, it would take a miracle to save her. By the time he reached the water, he had kicked off his shoes and dropped his shirt in the sand. Unsure of his direction, he started wading into the ocean when a distance away, Ally's head suddenly broke the surface of the water. Relief made him weak.

There was a collective gasp from the gathering

crowd behind him and then someone shouted, "She's got him!"

But East was already up to his waist and moving fast. He dove headfirst into an oncoming wave and started swimming.

Sunlight pierced the fluid world in which Ally was swimming, and yet she could not see clearly enough to give her a direction in which to search. Treading water beneath the surface, she turned in a complete circle, searching for a flash of red or a shadow that might be the child, himself. Her lungs were burning and the salt water had all but blinded her, yet she couldn't bring herself to give up.

Then she saw something drifting down to her right and moved swiftly toward it. Suddenly, her hand brushed against flesh, then fabric. It was the little boy's shorts. With one desperate grab, she pulled, and moments later, felt the cold, lifeless impact of a tiny body against her chest. The need to inhale was overwhelming as she began to move toward the surface, ever closer toward the light and the life-giving air she knew was there. But the harder she kicked, the farther away it seemed to be. Just when she thought it was over, she broke the surface of the water, gasping for air with the child held fast against her.

Everything was a blur, but she could hear people shouting. She turned toward the sound and saw the dark, imposing shape of the coastline, took another deep breath and began to swim, pulling the little boy as she went. Suddenly, East was right before her, touching her, taking the burden of the child's lifeless body from her weary arms. She wanted to cry with relief.

"Are you all right? Can you make it back to shore?" East shouted.

She nodded.

"Are you sure?"

"Go, just go," she yelled.

East began to swim, pulling the child along like a small, deflating raft. When his feet finally touched bottom, he lifted the child into his arms and started running toward the beach. Hotel staff waded out to meet him and together, they soon had the child on the sand. He looked up at the crowd, then waved frantically toward the water at Ally.

"Help her."

A couple of men separated themselves from the crowd as East bent over the child. As he began CPR, the loud, insistent sound of an approaching siren could be heard coming up the mountain. And then his entire focus became that cold little body on the sand, and the feel of a tiny blue mouth beneath his lips.

Ally was all but dragged from the water. She managed to walk about a half-dozen steps when her legs gave way. With a low, weary groan, she waved away the men who'd helped her and dropped to her hands and knees with her head down, trying to catch her breath. Someone draped a blanket around her shoulders and murmured something in her ear, but it didn't register. She couldn't think past the sight of East bending over the baby.

"Please, God," she whispered. "Please. Don't let him die."

In the background, Ally was vaguely aware of an ambulance pulling to a stop at the top of the bluff, and then people in uniforms scrambling down the steps to get to the beach. But the silence that engulfed them was telling. There was nothing but the throb of the ocean behind them and the sun overhead. Even the seagulls seemed to sense the unfolding drama and had absented themselves from the sky in deference to the man and the child.

And then everything seemed to happen in slow motion.

There was a cough, then a gurgle, and East was turning the boy on his side as water came spilling out of his mouth. A mother's sob was undermined by a collective sigh of relief from the crowd as the child started to cry.

As the first paramedic came on the scene, East gladly relinquished the child to the expert and rocked back on his heels in exhaustion.

When the child started to cry, Ally started to shake— first from the chill, then from relief. He was alive. Thank God, he was alive. Unashamed of the tears on her cheeks, she lifted her face to the sun and began struggling to her feet. Suddenly, East was in front of her. Before she could speak, he pulled her into his arms and held her close against his chest, his voice rumbling low against her ear.

"You did it, Ally. You did it! You saved his life."

She grabbed his arms and pushed herself back. "No," she said fiercely. "We did it."

At that moment, East couldn't bring himself to speak.

Behind them, the paramedics were strapping the little boy into a basket-like stretcher and starting toward the stairs at the base of the cliff. The crowd moved with them, leaving East and Ally alone on the beach.

She shuddered and pulled the blanket a little closer

around her, but it wasn't enough. The chill was all the way to her bones.

East saw her muscles beginning to spasm, and concern for her health shifted his focus.

"You need to get out of those wet clothes and into something warm and dry."

He took her by the hand as they started toward the steps and she let him lead her as if she were a child. Halfway there, East stopped and picked up their shoes and shirts then glanced at her, as if assuring himself she was still upright.

As they started up the steps, East took her by the elbow, bracing her weight against his body. About halfway up, Ally's legs began to shake, but she kept on climbing, afraid if she stopped, she wouldn't be able to move. Twice East felt her falter, and each time, although he remained silent, the look he gave her was filled with concern. When they reached the top, Ally breathed a shaky sigh of relief. The worst was surely over.

"Ally?"

She managed a smile. "I'm fine," she said, and made it all the way through the lobby before she suddenly stopped and clutched at her pockets. "My room key. It was in my pocket!"

"Wait here," East said, and headed for the desk, returning moments later with a duplicate.

They made it all the way to the bank of elevators before she stumbled. East cursed beneath his breath, punched the button, dumped their shoes and shirts into her hands, and then scooped her into his arms.

"Don't argue," he muttered.

"I didn't say a word," she said, and then leaned her head against his chest, grateful for his strength.

The ride up the elevator was silent. Ally took one look at their reflection in the mirrored car and closed her eyes, unable to face the expression on her own face—or on his. There were emotions she didn't know how to explore without making a fool of herself, or embarrassing him. Moments later, the doors opened and East strode out with her still in his arms.

When they entered her suite, it was impossible to mistake the meaning of the packed suitcases by the door. He stifled a frown and kept on going to the bedroom. He set her down on the side of the bed, only to stalk out, returning shortly with both bags in his hands.

"You'll be needing dry clothes," he said. "Which one are they in?" She pointed to the larger bag. He set it on the bed and then started to leave when she stopped him with one word.

"Wait."

He turned. The look on her face said it all. Seconds later she was in his arms. Pressing kisses across her forehead, then her cheeks, he began to gain sanity only after he realized she hadn't slapped his face.

"God in heaven, I thought you were both—"

Ally put her fingers across his lips. "I'm tougher than I look."

He cupped her face with the palms of his hands, looking deep into her eyes. He saw her pupils dilate, then her lips part. He sighed, then lowered his head, aware that the inevitability of this moment had been upon him since the day he'd first seen her face.

She tasted of seawater and tears, and an innocence that scared him to death. When she leaned into him and moaned, a surge of need came fast. Then she shuddered, and he became aware of her bare skin and wet clothes and he made himself move away.

"You need to get out of those clothes before you get sick," he said, and then leaned down and gave her one last kiss.

She took the kiss as if it were a life-giving drink and wondered if she would survive leaving this man after all.

When he turned her loose, she looked away, suddenly embarrassed that she'd given away too much of herself.

East sighed. He didn't know whether he'd made the situation better or worse, but he did know he would do it again.

"It's going to be okay," he said, and picked up his shirt and shoes.

What's going to be okay? You? Me? Everything? Nothing?

"Oh, sure, I know that," she said, and tried to pretend that she could kiss a man—even if it was Easton Kirby—without coming undone.

"Take a hot shower and get into some dry clothes. When you come out, I'll have something to warm you inside, as well."

She nodded.

"I'm going to go down to the lobby and check with Foster, just to make sure everything is under control. I'll be right back."

"There's no need to—"

East frowned. "I have a need," he said shortly. "So don't argue."

Ally could hardly focus on her shower for thinking about East and needs. It wasn't until she heard the door slam that she remembered the picture. She shivered again. There would be time enough later to show him the picture and the note. Right now, she needed to be

warm. She dug through her suitcase, pulled out a clean
pair of pants and a shirt, and some fresh underwear,
then headed for the bath. It wasn't until she was completely undressed that she realized she needed her toilet
articles, which were also packed and in the living room.
Wrapping a bath towel around her nudity, she ran into
the living room and retrieved the small bag from the
floor. As she turned, she caught a flash of movement
through the French doors leading out to the terrace and
stopped to look, absently noting a large, and rather el-
egant yacht. It occurred to her then that she'd seen it
before and as she watched, the skin on the back of her
neck began to crawl. She glanced down at the picture
on the table and then back out the window.

Taken from the water. The picture had been taken
from the water. From a yacht? What if it had been that
one?

"Oh man," she mumbled, and dashed back into her
bedroom, frantically throwing clothes aside as she
searched for the binoculars she always carried.

Moments later she ran back in the living room with
the towel still clutched around her and the binoculars
in her hand. Her hands were shaking as she tried to
unlatch the exterior door and when it finally gave, she
burst out onto the terrace and lifted the binoculars to
her face.

It took several seconds before she had them adjusted
to the distance, and by then, the yacht was almost
around the point. She could see crew moving about,
but there were no identifying flags and no name on the
side of the boat. Before she could look any further, it
disappeared from sight.

Muttering beneath her breath, she retreated back inside and closed the door. It seemed highly unlikely that

a rich man should buy such a magnificent toy and then neglect to give it a name. And while she knew there were hundreds of boats that sailed up and down these shores in any given year, instinct told her this one had been different.

"Damn it," she muttered as she tossed the binoculars on the sofa and headed for a much-needed shower.

A short while later, she came out of the bath with the towel wrapped around her again, intent on getting into clean clothes. But she wasn't prepared for the man standing in her room, or the look on his face.

"Oh!" she gasped, clutching the towel a little tighter. "You startled me."

"What the hell is this about?" East asked, and tossed the picture and the note on the bed between them.

She sighed, then reached for her clothes. "You tell me," she said. "It was delivered to the desk this morning. A bellhop brought it up."

East thought of Jonah and his expression darkened. "This isn't good."

"Oh, I don't know," Ally drawled. "I thought they captured your best side. However, had I known, I might have worn a different dress. White rarely photographs well on me."

"Damn it, Ally, this is serious."

"It has to do with Jonah, doesn't it?"

A dark flush spread across his cheeks as he gave her a hard, angry stare.

"Just get dressed," he muttered, and stalked out of the room.

Her shoulders slumped as she dropped to the side of the bed. "So much for the hour of the heroine. Now it's back to being the bearer of bad news."

* * *

East was pacing when Ally walked into the living room. He stopped, picked up a glass of wine from the bar and thrust it into her hands.

"The something warm that I promised you," he muttered.

"Am I to drink it, or drown myself in it?" she drawled.

East jabbed his hands through his hair in an angry gesture, then took a deep breath and made himself calm.

"Look, there are things going on that you don't understand."

"Obviously."

"The picture…it blows your cover…not just for this little job you were sent to do, but for anything else…ever."

"Not necessarily," Ally said, and sniffed the wine before taking a sip. Then she wrinkled her nose and set the glass aside. "I like it sweeter."

"Two hundred and ninety-five dollars a bottle and she wants grape juice," East muttered, then pointed. "Drink the damn stuff anyway."

Ally lifted her chin in gentle defiance. "I may not be wise in the ways of lust and seduction, but I am intelligent enough to know when I don't want to drink. I am tough. I have been in worse situations. I will not succumb to pneumonia or faint."

She moved toward him until there was little but guesswork between them, then jabbed her finger into his chest. "What I do want are some answers. My career is on the line and I don't even know why."

"Ask Jonah."

"He's not here. I'm asking you."

East spun toward the window, his shoulders hunched against the truth of her words. Silence followed, then lengthened. When he finally turned around, it gave him a measure of satisfaction to see that she hadn't moved. In a way, it was the final proof for him that she had more than her intelligence. She had staying power. It was a good trait.

"This changes everything. We need to talk to Jonah," East said.

"Are you going to help him?" Ally asked.

East frowned. "I don't know."

Ally shrugged and moved toward the front door. "Let me know when you do."

East's eyebrows rose. "Where the hell are you going?"

"To get something to eat. I'm starving. Oh, and by the way, the little boy…is he going to be all right?"

East nodded. "Yes. His parents called from the hospital. The boy is in observation, but he's not in any imminent danger."

"That's one good thing for the day, isn't it, East?"

Ally managed a smile. It wasn't much as smiles go, but there was a yearning in it that East couldn't ignore.

"Yes," he said. "It's a very good thing."

She held out her hand. "I'm going to the restaurant now. May I have my new key?"

East dug into his pocket and then handed it over. "So, does this mean you're staying?"

She gave him a slow, studied look and then dropped the key into her pocket.

"Only until you make up your mind—one way or the other."

* * *

Jeff came to in the dark just long enough to realize he couldn't move. Disoriented and sick to his stomach, he had no idea what was happening to him. Then he began to separate other sounds from the rough gasp of his own breath. He was inside a moving vehicle, and from the sound of the high-pitched whine of tires on pavement, moving at a rapid rate of speed. His stomach rolled, and he took a deep breath, willing himself to hang on. He thought about friends at school, his co-workers at the hospital, and then he thought about his dad and wondered if he'd ever see any of them again. Before he could dwell on his situation, the drug that they'd given him pulled him back under and he gratefully gave up the fight.

The next morning, Ally woke to a gray, overcast day. Just the lack of sunshine was enough to make her roll over in bed and try for another hour of sleep. But as soon as she closed her eyes, her mind began to stir. It had been almost twenty-four hours since the picture and the note had been delivered to her room and she had yet to contact Jonah, because when she did, she knew he would pull her out. And therein lay the rub. She didn't want to go. As long as she pretended to herself that East was going to change his mind, it gave her a reason to stay.

She buried her nose in the pillow and squeezed her eyes tight, trying to reclaim the memory of his mouth upon her lips and his hands centered in the middle of her back, but it wouldn't come. She rolled over on her back with a groan and stared up at the ceiling, trying to figure out what it was about the man that was making her nuts. She had seen plenty of good-looking men before and never been bothered with her emotions getting out of control. But with East, it was as if she'd lost every ounce of good sense she'd been born with. Rationally, she knew he was out of her league, but it didn't stop her from wanting, and oh, how she wanted.

Finally, she got up and stomped toward the bathroom. Maybe a hot shower and some food would put her world back on center. A short while later she stopped in the living room and gave herself the once-over before she went down to eat.

Her clothes were nondescript—a pair of well-worn jeans, a white, long-sleeved cotton sweater and her favorite pair of sandals. The only colors on her body were her red toenails and a pale peach gloss on her lips. Her gaze moved to her hair. It was its usual auburn cap of flyaway curls and nothing she could do anything about. With a shrug, she put her key in her pants pocket and slung her purse over her shoulder, then left the suite.

As she exited the elevator, she automatically looked toward the desk, hoping she might see East. He was nowhere in sight. She kept on walking, telling herself it didn't matter. When she exited the lobby onto the terrace, a sharp breeze almost took her breath away and she did a quick about-face and chose to eat indoors, instead.

She was seated at a table by the window and giving her order to a waiter, when East suddenly appeared.

"Eating alone?" he asked.

She handed the waiter her menu as he left, then focused her gaze on East. It had been more than twenty-four hours since they'd spoken and she was a little surprised by his presence.

"Not if you join me," she said.

He pulled out the chair to her left and sat with his back to the view.

"Didn't you want to order something?" she asked.

"I already did."

She arched an eyebrow. "Pretty sure of yourself, aren't you?"

He shrugged. "If I wasn't here, I'd be somewhere else. They would have found me."

Ally dropped her elbows onto the table and then rested her chin in her hands.

"Got anything you want to tell me?"

He stifled a smile as he reached for his napkin, unfolding it carefully, then draping it across his slacks.

"We're out of peanut butter."

She laughed and the sound dragged itself across East's emotions. He'd never heard her laugh before—not like this—uninhibited and all the way from her gut.

Still chuckling, she shuffled through her place setting of silverware and absently dropped her napkin in her lap.

"Okay, I get the message, but I've got one for you. I'm leaving tomorrow, with or without you."

East's heart skipped a beat. He'd gotten too used to seeing her around. The last twenty-four hours had been some of the emptiest times of his life and the thought of never seeing her again seemed impossible to consider. Within a very few days, she'd become someone special. It shouldn't have happened. He'd been so careful over the years to stay clear of emotional entanglements and now he felt ties to a woman he'd done nothing but kiss—and only once at that. If a single kiss could tie him in knots, he shuddered to think what would happen if they ever made love.

"Look, I—" In the middle of a word, his cell phone rang. "Excuse me," he said, and took the call.

"This is Kirby."

"And this is your worst nightmare," a man said.

East stiffened. "Who is this?"

"It's not my identity that matters. It's the identity of my hostage that you should be concerned with."

"What are you saying?" East muttered, then stood abruptly and walked toward the solitude of the terrace, unaware that Ally was right behind him.

"We've got your kid, and if you want to get him back alive, then you'd better do as I say."

East's mind went blank. Jeff? Someone had kidnapped Jeff? If this was so, he needed to catch them off guard. He laughed, a cold, ugly bark that ripped up his throat as he stepped out onto the terrace facing the wind.

"Look, you lying son of a bitch, I don't believe you."

"Just give your kid a call. See if he answers the phone," the man said.

East was thinking fast, laying a bet with himself that the kidnappers wouldn't have known Jeff's schedule well enough to know when East was bluffing.

"Hell, no. He's not going to answer his phone because he's backpacking up in the hills and won't be home for a good three days, so don't pull that crap on me."

Then, before he could change his mind, he disconnected, fully aware that he was gambling with Jeff's life.

"Ah, God," he groaned, and covered his face. What if he'd just signed his son's death warrant?

Ally grabbed him by the arm. "What?" she cried. "What's happening?"

East turned, then looked down at the phone in his hand as if it had become something foul.

"I think someone's kidnapped my son."

Chapter 7

Ally gasped. First the picture and the note—now this. They should have been expecting something more to occur, but how could they have guessed it would affect his son? She thought of the phone in her dresser.

"We've got to tell Jonah," she said and started to leave when East grabbed her by the arm.

"No! We wait. I just gambled my son's life on the hope that they would let me talk to him just to prove he was there."

Ally nodded as her estimation of Easton Kirby rose. That was a tough call to make, but one of the gutsiest moves she'd ever seen. And as she watched his face getting paler by the moment, she knew it was costing this man way more than he had to lose. She laid her hand in the middle of his back.

"Then we wait."

East turned toward the sea, his knuckles white from the death grip he had on the railing. "Now do you

understand why I told Jonah no? This is a perfect ex-
ample of why I refused him. You can't have a family
and be in this business. If it doesn't kill you, it will
damn sure kill them.''

Ally had no answer because she knew it was the
truth. And the wait continued…

Less than five minutes later, East's phone rang. The
moment he answered, he accepted the fact that he was
mixed up in Jonah's mess now, whether he wanted it
or not.

''This is Kirby,'' he said shortly.

A soft chuckle rippled through his ear and sent shock
waves of panic skittering through his mind.

''And a gutsy bastard, too, aren't you?''

''Who are you?'' East snapped.

''I'm not important, but the people who have your
son are not your usual society-page gentlemen, so I
strongly suggest you don't hang up on me again.''

''If they have my son as you claim, then somebody
better be proving it to me, and I don't mean some recorded little bit of his voice,'' East snapped. ''That
proves nothing about his still being alive. I want to talk
to him, and I want to ask questions that only he can
answer, or we have nothing to discuss.''

''You're not calling the shots,'' the man said. ''I am.
And it will be proven to you all too soon. However,
let me outline what it is that I want from you before
we hang up. That way when you get your call, you will
already know where we stand.''

''I'm listening,'' East growled.

''I want Jonah,'' the man whispered, and the hate in
his voice was impossible for East to mistake.

''What the hell do you expect me to do about it?''

East said. "I have no idea who or where he is. No one does."

"But you know how to contact him," the man said. "And I know that he's contacted you. I also know that he's sent you a pretty little helper to bring me down, but it isn't going to happen."

The information the man unwittingly gave was important, because it told East that the man wasn't as thorough as he believed himself to be. Ally hadn't come to help, she'd come to talk him into something he'd already refused.

"So what?" East said. "Just because I could talk to him, means nothing. I have no way of ferreting information out of a ghost."

The man chuckled again. "Ghosts aren't as elusive as one might think. However, that's not the point. The point is, you will work with me, getting me certain information and I will take it from there."

East inhaled slowly. "You expect me to steal documents and information that would point back to Jonah as being the thief? That could take weeks, even months to set up."

"I knew you were a smart man. You catch on fast, and you don't have weeks or months to do it. I'm no longer a patient man."

"I won't do it."

"Yes, you will, if you want to see your son alive."

"I don't know that you even have him."

"You will," the man snapped, suddenly tired of the game. "And know this, I will be calling you again and when I do, you'd better have what I want."

Startled by the abruptness of the disconnect, he inhaled sharply, then turned toward Ally, his jaw set and clenched. "Son of a bitch. The sorry, son of a bitch. He shouldn't have messed with what's mine."

At that moment, Ally knew that in his mind, Easton Kirby had already vaulted the distance from hotel manager back to an agent for SPEAR. But he wasn't doing it for Jonah.

Jeff had been awake for what seemed like hours, although he couldn't be sure. Without anything to help him gauge time or distance, he had no idea how long he'd been unconscious or where the kidnappers were taking him. At first, he'd been unable to understand why he'd be anyone's target for ransom. He didn't have money and neither did his dad—at least not that kind of money. With the passing of time, the drug began to lose its control and with cognizance came clearer thinking.

It occurred to him that he might have been snatched because of what his dad used to do. East had never elaborated on it, and Jeff had known not to ask, but he did know that his father used to be a spy of sorts. He couldn't help thinking that he had become the pawn in an ugly game of payback. And while he knew the deduction was pretty far-fetched, so was the fact that he'd been abducted. However, he didn't think he was in immediate danger of being killed. At least not yet. If that had been the case, they would have done it sooner and certainly closer to home. Why take the risk of being stopped by a highway patrol and being discovered in possession of a bound man in a trunk?

A short while later, the van took a sharp turn. Unable to brace himself, the trunk slid and Jeff slid with it, slamming his face against the trunk with a thump. Stunned by the unexpectedness of the pain, he groaned as the wounds on his already swollen mouth reopened. Cursing the driver and the world in general, he spit blood and prayed for the ride to end.

The ride then became a constant series of jarring bumps, leading him to assume they were now on a dirt road. He tried to measure time in the hope he could gauge some kind of distance, but was without success. It seemed endless and he was in desperate need of water, and a bathroom.

Just when he thought his misery would never end, the van rolled to a stop, and the moment it did, Jeff's heart skipped a beat. Had he guessed wrong about them keeping him alive? Was this the end after all? When he heard their voices, and then the sound of the door sliding back on the van, he braced himself for the worst.

Thin, gray clouds scattered themselves across the sky like trailing threads from an unraveling piece of fabric, forming a dramatic backdrop for the man who strode out of the weathered frame house in the middle of the Brotherhood compound. Caleb Carpenter was tall and rangy with piercing blue eyes and hair that was as short and dark as his temper. He glared at the trio getting out of the van.

"Elmore, where the hell have you been? You're four hours late."

Elmore Todd jerked to attention. "Sir, it wasn't our fault. There was some sort of roadblock outside of Reno. We had to take another route to safeguard the target."

"Roadblock? What kind of roadblock?"

The second kidnapper, who called himself Beau, backed up Elmore's explanation.

"It had nothing to do with us, Caleb, I swear. We heard later on the radio that they were looking for some crazy carjacker who'd killed a woman and her kid."

The last one, a skinny misfit of a man who answered to the name of Phil, added his two cents to the story.

"Yeah, and can you beat it? The car he jacked was a lousy hunk of metal. You'd think if you was gonna kill for a car, you'd have the sense to pick one that was worth something."

Resisting the urge to deck Phil on general principles, Caleb pivoted sharply and motioned to the men behind him.

"Get that trunk out of the van now! I need to see what we're dealing with here." And then he fixed the three with a hard-edged stare. "And the goods better be in pristine condition as requested, or someone's going to be sorry."

Elmore paled. "He put up a hell of a fight."

Caleb's lips thinned into a grimace of a smile. "There were three of you and one of him, what the hell kind of a fight could he make?"

"Well, you said his daddy was some kind of a Fed. He must have been the one who taught him all that karate." Beau blustered, and hawked and spit just to give himself time to think. Then he added, "Besides, I never did trust a man who fought with his feet 'stead of his fists."

Caleb cursed beneath his breath as he pointed to the trunk that was now on the ground.

"Open it," he ordered.

The lid came up, revealing the man within. The first thing Caleb saw was fresh blood. He doubled his fist and pivoted sharply, nailing Elmore Todd in the nose. Blood spurted, rocking the man back on his heels. The other two took a nervous step backward, afraid they were next. To their relief, Caleb seemed to be through distributing punishment.

"Next time I send you on a mission, I expect orders to be followed."

"Yes, sir," Elmore muttered, and clamped a handkerchief over his mouth and nose to staunch the flow.

"Get him out," Caleb said, pointing toward the man in the trunk.

Moments later, Jeff Kirby found himself face-to-face with the man in charge. His legs were numb and kept threatening to fold and his throat was tight and scratchy, but he was in so much misery and pain that he was past being scared. He squinted at the man they called Caleb through a half-swollen eye.

"I want a drink of water and a bathroom, and not in that order."

Caleb Carpenter froze. The last thing he'd expected was a victim making demands. And what a pitiful victim he was—both fresh and dried blood dotted his clothing, and his face was swollen and bruised. Yet still bound, the kid was staring him straight in the eye.

A slow grin spread across Caleb's face. "The hell you say," he said softly, then pointed to the man nearest him. "You heard the man. Get that damned tape off his hands and feet and take him to the john, then get him a drink. He's thirsty."

Later, Jeff would look back on that moment and realize how fortunate he'd been in not getting himself shot. Every man there had been wearing some kind of uniform and was armed to the teeth. And the tattoo he'd seen on the man they called Elmore was on posters all over the place. Added to that, all of the vehicles in the compound had Idaho plates. At least now he

knew where he was—sort of—and he knew his kidnappers' faces. But that last bit of knowledge was what
worried him most. Granted he was still alive, and with
a fresh meal starting to digest in his belly, but if they
planned to let him go at some future date, then why
had they let him see their faces?

Later, he paced the small, six-by-six room that
they'd locked him in until his legs ached and the bot-
toms of his feet began to burn. Exhausted, he dropped
onto the single piece of furniture in the room, an old
army cot, and stretched out. How in hell would anyone
ever find him in this godforsaken place? He might as
well be on the moon.

Time passed and the air began to chill as the day
turned to night. He huddled upon the cot without benefit of blankets until anger resurfaced, then he crawled
off the cot and began pacing to stay warm.

Caleb Carpenter was on a mission. The phone call
he'd just received left him with a rather nasty task to
perform. And while it was a bit unexpected, he had not
argued with the man who'd given the order. It would
seem that the father of the kidnap victim wasn't being
as pliable as they'd expected. He had demanded proof
that his son was still alive and well, or they could all
go to hell. Although they were on different sides of the
war, there was a part of Caleb Carpenter that admired
that kind of grit. What he had to do, however, was
make sure that the kid didn't give anything away, and
that was what worried him. Jeff Kirby was acting more
like an unhappy guest at a cut-rate motel, rather than
a victim. Caleb shook his head in disgust as he headed
toward the makeshift armory where Jeff was being
held. It was a shame that their need for money to fund

their program had thrown them in with such a despicable despot. Kidnapping wasn't Caleb's chosen method of protesting and in his opinion, there wasn't one admirable thing about the man behind this mess. The Brotherhood of Blood operated on the age-old principles of the right to bear arms and a refusal to bow down to an oppressive government, while the man with the money seemed bent on nothing but personal revenge. It was not a trait Caleb found admirable or productive. But they'd taken the money and therefore, would do the job. He was not a man who went back on his word.

As he strode into the armory, two of the men on guard jumped to their feet.

"Morning, sir," they said, and all but stood at attention.

He nodded, then pointed toward the locked door. "Open it and bring him out."

They did as they were told, entering together, then coming out moments later with the young man clutched between them.

Caleb eyed the man's wounds, judging them to be healing, then motioned for Jeff to come forward.

"You, come here," he said.

"The name's Jeff."

Caleb's eyes narrowed thoughtfully. The kid was slick, he'd give him that. Being on a first-name basis was the first step in bonding. Maybe he thought it would make it easier to stay alive.

"You've got a phone call to make," Caleb said. "And if you want your daddy to keep breathing, you won't try to be a smart-mouth and give away something you shouldn't, understand?"

Jeff's pulse skittered, then settled. "You want me to talk to him?"

Caleb nodded.

"It seems he doesn't trust our accommodations and wants to make sure we have clean sheets on the bed."

To Caleb's surprise, Jeff pulled his swollen lips into what passed as a grin, upping his admiration for the young man even more. Without giving away any of his thoughts, he dialed the number that had been given him, then waited for Easton Kirby to answer.

When the phone rang, East stiffened, then let it ring again.

Ally stared. "East?"

On the third ring, he answered, his voice deep and angry, his words clipped.

"This is Kirby."

Caleb Carpenter shifted his stance, reminding himself that the man on the other end was not the one in control.

"You wanted to speak with your son, make it brief, and don't forget I'll be listening." Then he thrust the phone at Jeff. "Remember what I said."

Jeff took the phone. "Dad?"

East's knees buckled, but there was no other indication of how deeply he was moved.

"Did they hurt you?" he asked.

"Not enough to count."

East cursed. "Are they listening?"

"Like vultures."

East sighed. "I'm so sorry this happened to you."

"Yeah, I really crashed and burned this time, didn't I, Dad? Unlike you, I won't be able to walk out of this on my own."

East's pulse jumped. Jeff was trying to tell him something, but what?

"Don't give up on me, boy. I'll get you out. I swear to God, I'll find a way."

Caleb yanked the phone from Jeff's hand. "Sorry, Daddy, but your change just ran out. Now I suggest you do as the big man ordered if you want your son back alive."

He punched the button and disconnected.

East dropped the phone into his pocket and turned to face Ally.

"What did Jeff say?" she asked. "Is he all right? Did they hurt him?"

"I'll tell you everything later. Now we call Jonah."

She sighed. This was not how it was supposed to be. "In my room," she said shortly.

He followed her toward the elevators, while hundreds of miles away, Caleb Carpenter was putting his own set of plans into motion. He turned to his men.

"It's time," he said, pointing toward Jeff. "Put him in the hole."

The hole? Jeff spun, bracing himself for another unknown, but it was no use. He was surrounded by armed men and with nowhere to go but where he was led. They stopped about a hundred yards away from the main cluster of buildings and began moving aside a camouflage net lying across a stack of boxes. When Jeff saw the metal door beneath, he stifled a groan.

The door opened silently on well-oiled hinges, revealing a steep set of steps leading into a dark, ominous cavern.

Jeff frowned. *Another dark hole? What is it with these people and lights?*

"Get in," Elmore said, and gave Jeff a sharp push.

He staggered forward, then took his first step down.
"Hurry up. We ain't got all day."

Jeff braced himself with both hands as he started
down the stairs.

"Where's the light?" he asked.

"You get a minute to orient yourself and then the
door goes shut, so stop talking and start looking."

Jeff's heart skipped a beat as an old memory from
his childhood suddenly surfaced. There was a man—
an angry man—shoving him into a closet and slamming the door. He could remember the feel of old shoes
beneath his hands and the scent of dust and leather.

Not this. God, not this.

But as Jeff reached the bottom of the steps and began
to look around, it became all too obvious that this was
real. There was a commode, a cot, a large water can,
and a small, spindly table stacked with some sort of
containers of non-perishable food inside a concrete-
lined hole barely tall enough for him to stand. He
caught a glimpse of a small, narrow tube poking
through the ceiling and assumed it was an air vent, then
saw a logo on one of the small containers just as the
door began to shut. MRE—meals ready to eat. If it
hadn't been so dismal, he would have laughed. Again,
his creature comforts were going to be compliments of
army surplus and Uncle Sam. He wondered if his dad
would get the clue that he'd been trying to send, and
then they closed the door and everything went black.

East shut the door abruptly as they entered Ally's
room.

"How do you contact him?" he asked.

"Wait here," Ally said, and dashed toward her bedroom, coming back moments later with the phone that

Jonah had sent her. She pressed the Send button as instructed, let it ring two times, then disconnected.

"Now we wait," she said.

East had worked too many years under Jonah to question the procedures. Instead, he began to pace.

"You don't tell him what's happened to Jeff."

Ally's mouth dropped. "But—"

"No!" East said, raising his voice. "If he knows, he'll put somebody else on the case because it's become too personal for me."

"But isn't it?" Ally asked.

"Hell, yes," East said. "And that's exactly why I'm doing it. Not for him. Not for Uncle Sam."

"Then what do you tell him?" she asked. "And you'd better decide quickly, because he'll be calling within the minute."

"As far as you know, I have decided to help. You tell Jonah that, then let me talk. After that, you can go on to your next assignment and leave the rest of this mess to me."

Ally's face turned a quick, angry red. "Leave? Now? What kind of a person do you think I am?"

East paused, surprised by her vehemence. "This is no longer any of—"

"You can't do this by yourself and you know it," she snapped. "You've been out of the business too long. Besides, don't forget my intelligence. Use it. Use me. However, whenever. Just let me help."

East's expression shifted. Not much, but enough to let Ally know that she'd gotten to him. For now, it was enough. Before they could go any further, the phone suddenly rang.

"Answer it," East said. "Then tell him I want to talk."

Ally put the phone to her ear. "Hello, this is Corbin."

A deep, gravely voice rattled across Ally's eardrum. "Talk to me."

"He's in."

Ally heard a swift intake of breath, and then a moment of silence.

"Sir? Are you there? He wants to talk."

"Yes. Of course. Put him on."

She handed the phone to East.

"Jonah, you are a persuasive man."

"I'm sorry it became necessary," Jonah said.

East bit back an angry retort. "Yes, so am I," he muttered. "However, down to business. I'll need information on everything that has occurred to date. Get it to me. Also, I may need some vital information from you later. If so, I will track the transmissions in hopes of finding the source."

Jonah frowned. This wasn't what he had planned. "I don't think—"

East interrupted. "You haven't been successful so far, so why not try things my way?"

Silence lengthened into a quiet that began to make East nervous. If Jonah didn't go for this, then how could he bargain with the kidnapper to buy Jeff some time?

"Done," Jonah finally said. "But do you have the expertise to—"

"Your messenger. I'm keeping your messenger."

This time, Jonah was silent for an even longer time. Finally, he spoke. "Why her?"

"You trusted her," East said. "And so do I."

"But she doesn't know why she was sent to persuade you."

"She will before we start, or it won't work."

Jonah's hesitation was brief. "All right, but you know the drill."

A cold smile broke the somberness of East's expression, although Ally was the only one to see it.

"Oh yeah, I know the drill," East said. "If caught or captured, it's my head on a platter, not yours, because you do not exist."

"I will be in touch," Jonah said.

"By this phone?"

"Yes. Now put Agent Corbin back on the phone."

East handed the phone to Ally. "He wants to talk to you."

"Sir?"

"He needs help," Jonah said. "Whatever he asks, whatever it takes, it's his."

"And that includes me?" Ally asked.

"Yes."

Ally hid a quick sigh of relief. "I'll do what I can."

"Let it be enough," Jonah said, and hung up.

Chapter 8

East moved through the dining area, then the lobby, heading toward his office with Ally in tow.

"Now tell me what Jeff said," she demanded.

East lowered his voice as they continued to move down a hallway past a series of rooms.

"He said something odd about having crashed and burned, then added that he wouldn't be able to walk out of it like I did. I think he was trying to tell me something, but I'm not sure what."

"Crash and burn? Have you ever been in a wreck?"

"We'll talk inside," he said, as they reached his office. East opened the door, stepping aside, letting her enter first. Once the door was firmly shut, he strode toward his desk and picked up the phone.

"Stella, have all of the business calls routed to Foster's office. I don't want to be disturbed."

"Yes, sir," the operator said.

East hung up.

"Wrecks. We were talking about wrecks," Ally prompted.

East sighed in frustration. "Yes, but which one? I've been in several car wrecks, a couple of plane wrecks, and even one train wreck."

Ally stared. "What are you...your own bad luck charm? Good grief, it's not that you've endured all that so much as you're still here to tell the tale."

East shrugged. "Occupational hazard."

"So how many of those crashed and burned."

A frown creased his forehead. "Maybe three...no four, counting that chopper that went down up north."

She had confiscated a piece of paper from his desk and was furiously writing as he continued to speak.

"And of those, how many did you walk away from?" she asked.

East was beginning to appreciate the beauty of Ally Corbin's mind.

"Two."

"And they were where?"

"A car wreck in upstate New York and a chopper crash in southern Idaho."

"New York and Idaho, two possibles," Ally muttered.

"Those are far-fetched assumptions."

"There's no law against assuming," she countered. "Besides, it's more than you had five minutes ago."

He shook his head and almost smiled. "What did Jonah tell you when he sent you here?"

"My mission was to persuade you to change your status with SPEAR from inactive to active."

"He didn't tell you why, or give you any deadlines?"

"No."

East combed his fingers through his hair in frustration, then began to pace.

"Look," Ally said. "I said I'd help, and I will. In fact I want to. I feel as if, in some way, my coming here has precipitated what has happened to your son."

East shook his head. "No, it wasn't just your appearance, although it's a part of the whole. It started with the reason for Jonah's request."

"What reason?"

East hesitated, then shoved aside his reluctance to break his silence. Jonah's situation was secondary to getting Jeff back safe and he'd do whatever it took to make that happen.

"Someone is trying to take Jonah down, and if they succeed, they'll take SPEAR with him."

Ally's mouth dropped. "Oh my God, you can't be serious!" Then she gave herself a quick thump on the forehead. "That's a stupid thing to say. I'm sorry. Please continue."

"A couple of weeks ago I got a phone call from Jonah. He told me of several recent incidents of people being arrested for treason that all pointed back to him."

"Is this national or global?" Ally asked.

"I got the impression that it was global," East said. "I'll know more when I get the file on the incidents. I think it's only a matter of time before his anonymity is blown and he's arrested, unless he can find out who's trying to discredit him. Because of the nature of the things that were being done, he had reason to suspect everyone, even the people within his organization."

Ally's expression lightened as understanding dawned. "And because you've been out of the loop, so to speak, he felt safe in assuming it wouldn't be you."

East nodded. "But I refused—for a number of reasons, not the least of which was this monkey of guilt I've had on my back for ten years. Back in my operative days, I accidentally killed a kid on a bike during a high-speed chase. It was ruled accidental, but it didn't change the fact that the kid was dead. Just thinking about returning to that life made me sick to my stomach. I didn't want to be responsible for another innocent's death."

Ally hurt for the pain she saw in his eyes and impulsively put her hand on his forearm. "I knew about that. Everyone in the department knows why you left and no one blames you. But you do know it wasn't your fault."

"Knowing and accepting are two different things. And there was Jeff. I'd adopted him after I'd taken this job. I couldn't see jeopardizing what family life I have now to go back underground. Not even for Jonah."

Ally sighed. "If I came across too militant before, I apologize. I didn't understand."

"You were only doing your job and Jonah is desperate and with good reason. But the son of a bitch who wants Jonah is obviously willing to sacrifice anyone to get the job done. Somehow he found out that Jonah had come to me, and when you showed up a short while later, I suppose he assumed we'd be working together to track him. He said as much when he called."

Ally shook her head. "That doesn't make sense. There are less than half a dozen people within the entire government that even know of SPEAR's existence. That should narrow the field."

"You're forgetting the people within the organization, itself. Add a good two hundred names to the list and we're getting close.''

"But we don't even know who Jonah is. How could anyone possibly have a grudge against a man we don't know?''

"That's just it," East said. "Someone does know who he is, and that someone has a personal axe to grind. The problem is, he's willing to bury anyone, including my son, to get what he wants.''

"How are you going to make this work? Won't Jonah suspect something? And even worse, what about the kidnapper? If he thinks you're trying to find Jeff…'' She stopped. "You are going to look for your son, aren't you?''

"Oh, yeah," East said. "Him and him alone. If the kidnapper happens to fall into the path, then so much the better for Jonah. But I have no intention of trying to take down a faceless man to save another faceless man—not even for God and country. As for Jonah, he's given me free rein, or at least he will, whether he knows it now or not. Bottom line…I'm going after Jeff, nothing more.''

Ally nodded. "Then that's what we'll do.''

It was the word *we* that got to him. East hadn't had anyone at his back for so long that the simple thought of not being alone brought him up short. He looked at Ally—really looked—for the first time since she'd revealed her true self, and saw, not the young, uncertain female she'd been, but a strong, confident woman willing to go the distance. This time it was he who reached out and touched. He cupped the side of her face with his palm, feeling the thread of a steady pulse beneath his thumb.

"Thank you.''

Ally's heartbeat fluttered. She had to remind herself that this wasn't a precursor to intimacy, but rather a gesture of thanks.

"I haven't done anything to help you yet," she said. "But I can promise you I will."

"You're wrong," he said softly. "You're here. That's what counts."

It came before daybreak; a fat, red, white and blue package by overnight express and East knew when he opened it that he was opening the proverbial can of worms. But what was inside was immaterial to where he was going. He'd delegated all his duties to Foster Martin the night before without a worry. Foster had shown an amazing change of character since the child's rescue from the sea, and the fact that he'd restrained from questioning East's decision to leave him in charge gave East a small measure of relief.

Afterward, East had gone to his apartment and packed for an indefinite leave of absence. But it was the knot in his gut and the gun in his suitcase that kept him awake most of the night. Every time he closed his eyes, he saw his son's face. It was all he could do to wait until dawn to head for L.A. And even though he'd tossed and turned, there was one redeeming fact that had kept him just that little bit sane; the knowledge that he wasn't facing this alone. But morning had come, and with it the packet he'd been waiting for.

Now, he tossed the file into his bag, zipped it shut, then reached for the phone. Ally answered on the first ring.

"I'm ready," she said.

"Meet you downstairs."

They hung up without saying goodbye and headed

for the door, each focused on their own agenda. East was going to what he assumed would be the scene of the crime, and Ally was going to pick it apart. Between them, they would surely find something that would give them a place to start.

It was almost noon by the time they reached L.A. Traffic was jammed on the exit that East normally used, forcing him to drive on, and he muttered beneath his breath knowing that it would take longer to back-track to Jeff's apartment.

"What a mess," Ally said.

"That's L.A."

"When I have a home, it's not going to be in a city," she muttered, and cast a wary eye out the window as they drove past a man and a woman who were standing on the shoulder of the road and screaming at each other beside a stalled car.

East gave her a curious look, then returned his attention to the traffic, but it had set a picture in his mind that he couldn't shake. Ally in a kitchen. Ally in a garden. Ally rocking babies.

He blinked. Where the hell had that last one come from? He decided to change subjects.

"What's your favorite food?" he asked. "Besides waffles with peanut butter and jelly, that is?"

"Anything, as long as it's not raw meat or made out of tofu, why?"

East grinned. "A woman after my own heart. And I asked because I'm starving. If I know Jeff, there will be nothing in his refrigerator but beer and a piece of week-old pizza." His grin faded. "I was coming up next week for a visit. He wanted steak."

Ally didn't take her eyes off the road. "We'll find

him,'' she said. ''Do you want to eat now, or go straight to Jeff's apartment?''

''Now's good, why?''

She pointed to a sign up ahead. ''How about barbeque?''

He swerved into the right-hand lane and began to slow down. Moments later, they were out of the car and following the aroma of hickory-smoked meat. Ally tripped as she started to step up the curb and East grabbed her.

''You all right?'' he asked, clutching her arm as he turned her to face him.

There was concern in his eyes as he waited for her answer, and all the while Ally was trying to form the word, she couldn't help thinking that once he'd looked at her with a different expression on his face.

''Ally?''

''Yes, of course. Just clumsy, I guess,'' and quickly pulled away before she made a fool of herself all over again.

East frowned as he followed her into the restaurant. To his surprise, they were seated almost immediately and he soon forgot the moment as they sat down.

''I hope this is a sign, because this is a first,'' he said.

''What's a first?''

''Since we've met, you fixed the hotel computer, saved a little boy's life and the hotel from a possible lawsuit, and now we've just walked into an L.A. eatery at noontime without a reservation and were seated without a wait. I'm thinking that you're my lucky charm.''

''There's no such thing as luck.''

''Excuse me?''

"It's all about the law of averages—you know, being in the right place at the right time. It has nothing to do with luck."

He leaned across the table and took her by the hand.

"It's difficult for you, isn't it?"

She looked down at her menu, pretending to study it as she spoke.

"What's difficult?"

"Accepting compliments."

"No, I don't think—"

"Ally."

She sighed, then laid her menu down and looked up. "What?"

"This may offend you, but in my opinion, your parents need a swift kick in the butt."

It was the last thing she had expected him to say. Her eyes widened and her lips parted, but for the life of her, she couldn't think of a thing to say. All she could do was savor the knowledge that someone cared—and not about what she could do, but about the way that she felt. Struggling with her emotions, she began to scan the menu anew and found herself looking at the words through a blur.

"Do you know what you want?" East asked.

She looked up, the word *you* on the tip of her tongue, and then nodded.

"I'll have the chopped brisket in a sandwich, an order of fries and a gallon of iced tea."

"Gallon?"

She pursed her lips. "A mere figure of speech." She pointed to a small pitcher of sauce sitting between a pair of salt and pepper shakers. "I can tell by the scent of the sauce that it's hot."

"Is that okay?" he asked.

"Oh, yes, I like it hot."

East's mind went blank and he was still staring at what looked to be a small freckle on the right side of her mouth when a waiter appeared to take their order.

The closer they came to Jeff's apartment, the tighter the knot drew in East's gut. He had no idea what he'd find inside, nor was he even certain that this was where Jeff had been abducted, but it was a place to start. By the time they parked in the parking lot, he'd gone completely silent.

Ally could only imagine the fear that must be going through East's mind and when they got to the door of Jeff's apartment she knew she had to say something to break the tension between them.

"I have a forensics kit in my backpack. If need be, I can do a thorough sweep of the place."

East gave her a new look of appreciation, then nodded. "Yes, bring it in. We can't involve the police. Which reminds me, I've got to talk to someone at UCLA Medical Center, or they might put out a missing person's report on him and blow everything out of the water."

As they entered, East caught himself holding his breath as he flipped on the light switch with the end of a ballpoint pen so as not to disturb any fingerprints. He exhaled on a slow, angry breath. Even though the furniture was in place, he could see signs of destruction.

"There's broken glass beneath this chair," Ally said, squatting down and pointing to a couple of small, glistening shards. Without touching them, she gazed about the room, looking at everything from this level and then suddenly focused on a dark smudge below a desk near the wall.

"East." She pointed.

He moved in that direction, then squatted, briefly touching the edge of the smudge. It was dry and flaky, but he didn't have to test the stain for identification. He'd seen enough dried blood in his days to recognize it.

"Son of a bitch."

"It doesn't have to mean it was Jeff's," she said. "Remember, you've talked to him, so whatever happened to him was not life threatening."

He exhaled slowly, reminding himself that she was right, then stood abruptly. As he started to turn away, something about the smear caught his attention and he stepped to the side then looked at it again. Suddenly, his heart skipped a beat. There were letters traced in the blood.

"Ally, get over here. Tell me if you see what I see."

She stood, then hurried over to where East was standing.

"What?" she asked.

He shook his head. "Just look. Tell me what you see." Then he stepped aside to give her room.

Ally glanced at the smear then past it, thinking that East had seen something else, something that she'd missed. But it was quickly apparent that there was nothing beneath the desk but the smear. She stepped to one side for a different view, and almost immediately, a name appeared in the smudge.

"A name! He wrote a name in the blood!"

East nodded with satisfaction. At least he hadn't been imagining it.

"That first one is a *B* for sure," Ally said.

"And the second is definitely an *O,*" East added.

"But the last one isn't as clear. It looks a little bit like a *P*...no, maybe it's a—"

"It's a *B*," Ally said. "I think it's a *B,* too." Then she looked at East. "Bob? Does that make sense to you?"

"No," East said, frowning in frustration. "Who the hell is Bob? Damn, this couldn't be much more generic."

"It's still something," she said. "Don't touch anything else until I get back, okay? I'm going to get my camera and the forensics kit out of my bag."

She headed for the bag she'd dropped by the door, leaving East alone with his thoughts, and they weren't very good. As he moved about the room, he found a large amount of broken glass in a wastebasket, and the lamp sitting on the end table beside the sofa was missing a bulb. When he looked closer, he noticed that the base of a broken bulb was still screwed into the socket. Only the globe was missing. He stopped and pivoted about the room, searching walls, windows and doors. There was a blank space on the wall where a picture had once hung and what appeared to be another smear of blood on the doorjamb leading to the hall. This made no sense. Why go to all the trouble to kidnap someone and then try to clean up the place, as if it had not happened—especially when he'd already received a ransom demand?

As he stood, contemplating the oddity of the clues, it occurred to him again that the man who'd made the demands had not been the one who'd done the snatch. It was as if the people who'd physically taken Jeff had been acting under orders rather than playing it by ear. No one in the heat of the moment of a crime is going to stop and clean up the scene unless they've been told

to do so, or unless they're trying to wipe away fingerprints. And, too many things had been handled in the
act of cleaning up to let East believe that these crimi-
nals had not been wearing gloves. The kidnapping had
been too intricately planned. No one connected with
this was going to be that stupid.

Besides that, there were the phone calls he'd received—first those from the man who'd made the demands, then the one from Jeff, himself. And the time
between the calls was even more proof. If Jeff was with
the mastermind, then why the long lapses between
calls? The longer he stood there, the more certain he
became that Jeff was being held in one place, while
the real man behind the crime was in another.

"Got it!" Ally announced.

She began unpacking the kit, her expression a study
in concentration. Only once did she look up, and that
was to ask East a question.

"Are Jeff's fingerprints on file anywhere?"

East nodded. "Unfortunately, yes. Before I found
him, he'd had several run-ins with the police. Nothing
serious, but very typical, homeless-kid-on-the-street
stuff."

Ally nodded. "Good," she muttered, and set to
work.

As East watched, the irony of it hit him. The mere
fact that Jeff had ever been arrested would play an
integral part in a process of elimination that might help
them find his kidnappers, instead. Jeff's prints were on
file. If they got lucky, maybe the other prints would
belong to a known felon and they would have a place
to start looking.

Several hours passed before Ally was satisfied that
she'd gathered all the possible forensic evidence. She

and East had worked head-to-head, speaking only in short questions and answers while taking blood samples and dusting for fingerprints on every imaginable surface, including the glass shards East had found in the wastebaskets. But now they were through. Ally had a knot in the muscles between her shoulder blades, and the beginnings of a miserable headache. The tension lines between East's eyebrows had deepened perceptibly.

East glanced at his watch, surprised to see how long they'd been working. He stepped back as Ally strode past him, heading toward the mini-lab she'd set up on the kitchen table. He saw the strain on her face before he felt his own and knew that they would have to stop, at least for a while. Burning out before they'd barely started would do no one any good, especially Jeff. He followed her into the kitchen.

"Ally..."

She laid down the evidence bags she was carrying and readjusted her microscope before reaching for a chair, unaware that East had called her name.

He smiled crookedly, wondering what it would take to get her attention.

"Ally, I'm talking to you."

She bent down to get a fresh set of slides from her carryall when East grabbed her by the shoulders and spun her around.

She'd been so deep in thought that she'd almost forgotten she wasn't alone. His touch, then that slow, husky drawl startled her enough that she gasped.

"What?"

"Sorry. I didn't mean to scare you, but you've been tuning me out for quite some time now."

She flushed and then smiled an apology. "Sorry. I get so focused when I work that I've been accused of forgetting to breathe."

"Focus is good, but there's a time for everything, and I think we both need a break."

"But the—"

He put a finger on the center of her mouth, stopping her from finishing her sentence. He'd only meant to tease, but the slight tremble of those soft, shapely lips set his own head spinning. He looked down at her face, at the startled, almost fearful expression on her face, and he groaned.

"Don't look at me like I'm going to eat you alive," he said.

"Sometimes I think I'll die if you don't." The moment she said it, she paled. "I didn't mean to say that out loud," she muttered as she tore herself free from his grasp and reached for the slides once again. "You need to leave. I can't concentrate when you're standing over my shoulder."

But East didn't move. He was still digesting the slip of her tongue. Finally, he shook his head in wonder and touched the back of her head, fingering the feathery curls at the soft nape of her neck.

"You can fuss and prickle at me all you want, Ally, but you can't ignore what you said."

She looked up, glaring. "No, but if you were a gentleman, you would."

He tilted her chin until they were looking into each other's eyes.

"What if I don't want to ignore it?"

Suddenly, the room was filled with a different sort of tension. Her eyelids fluttered as she tried to swallow past a sudden knot in her throat.

"Then I don't know," she muttered.

"Want to learn?" he asked, his breath soft against her cheek.

"Education is a wonderful thing," Ally whispered, and lifted her lips to the kiss she saw coming.

It was a gentle coupling; founded on a new and tenuous partnership and companionable exhaustion. East wrapped his arms around her and pulled her close against his body.

Ally moaned deep in her throat as she felt her bones turn to mush.

East was the first to pull away, however reluctantly.

"You're a quick study, aren't you, Ally girl?"

Ally blinked, trying to focus on something besides the shape of his mouth. When she saw he was teasing gently, it gave her the nerve to tease back.

"I tend to absorb what I like a lot faster than the dull stuff."

He laughed. "Damn. An honest woman. I may be in more trouble than I thought."

Ally arched an eyebrow, her expression suddenly serious.

"So, you think I'm trouble?"

East's smile disappeared. "Oh, honey…I know it."

Chapter 9

Night had come to L.A., but judging from the traffic on the streets below Jeff's apartment, it seemed few, if any, people slept. Light from the streets shone in through the kitchen window, highlighting the clutter, as well as the microscope and slides that Ally had left on the table, and leaving the rest of the room in shadows. A small black bug skittered across the linoleum and slipped under a crack in the floor, from where it was unlikely to emerge, thanks to monthly visits from an exterminator service.

Down the hall, at the first door on the right, Ally lay wide-eyed and sleepless, thinking about the man on the living room sofa. What had happened between them earlier today? Was it nothing more than a symptom of shared troubles, or was something special developing between them? Afraid to hope—afraid to count on anything more than herself—she rolled over onto her side and closed her eyes.

A night wind was playing havoc with the palms outside, leaving dancing shadows on the walls opposite the sofa where East lay trying to sleep, but it wouldn't come. Tired and frustrated, he got up and headed toward the patio doors leading to the small terrace beyond. A single click sounded in the silence as he flipped open the lock. The doors slid silently aside as he moved onto the terrace overlooking the parking lot below. Compared to the view at Condor Mountain, this one left a lot to be desired, but East knew Jeff was happy here. All he could do was hope that he got to come back and enjoy it.

A siren sounded in the distance, and then another in the opposite direction, while down below an argument was in progress. He lowered his head and closed his eyes, whispering a brief but heartfelt prayer for his son's safety. When he turned around, Ally was standing in the door wearing an over-size MIT T-shirt and a pair of socks. In the dark, without makeup, she could have passed for thirteen. It made him feel like a dirty old man, because at that moment, he wanted nothing more than to take her in his arms.

"I got up to get a drink of water," she said.

"I can't sleep either," he muttered, and turned back to the skyline of L.A. "Hell of a place, isn't it?"

Ally moved to stand beside him, shoulders touching, sharing the night and the space.

"When I was little, I was afraid of people who lived their lives in the dark. Intellectually, I knew there were people like doctors and policemen, even firemen, who had to work no matter what time of day it was. But a part of me was convinced that they were really vampires who came out after the sun went down and disappeared during the day." She managed a lopsided grin. "I saw an old movie about werewolves and vampires when I was about six. I didn't grasp all the nuances, just enough to scare the bejesus out of me for a good ten years."

East laughed, and again, was surprised that he could. There was something so sweet about her lack of artifice that he couldn't help himself.

"You're good for me. Did you know that?" he asked.

Ally shook her head.

"Well, you are," he said, and gave her a quick hug. As he did, he felt her shiver. "Let's get back inside before we both get a chill."

He nodded, as he led the way back inside, and then locked the door behind them. "How about some coffee?"

"I'll pass," she said. "It would just keep me awake."

"You're already awake," East argued. "What's one cup going to hurt?"

Reluctant to admit that she was afraid of making a fool of herself again, it was all she could do to agree. She stood in the dark, watching as East walked into the kitchen and turned on the light. From the living room, she felt safe; secluded from his all-seeing eyes. Yet when he beckoned, she followed him into the light, like a moth to the flame. Morning could come none too soon. Oddly enough, after two cups of coffee, they both went to sleep. East dreamed of her laughter, and Ally dreamed of his arms, holding her tight.

Hundreds of miles away on a Colorado mountaintop, Jonah stood on the second-story balcony of his home, looking out at the darkness and the star-filled night.

The emptiness of the house behind him was nothing more than a reflection of his own life. Despite his power, he had no roots—no family. If he survived this mess he was in, his future still looked bleak. It was impossible not to think of what the last years of his life would be like when he gave up this job to someone else. He would be exactly what he was now, only older—a lonely, lonely man.

A deep sigh racked his body as he looked up at the sky. As he watched, a shooting star suddenly fell into his line of vision, disappearing as quickly as it had appeared, and as it did, an old memory suddenly re-surfaced. As a young man, he'd stood in the dark on a night like this and watched stars falling from heaven. Only he hadn't been alone. He shuddered, remembering the sequence of events that had taken him to where he was now and as he did, loneliness turned to a slow, simmering rage. He'd given up too damned much in the service of others. And as he stood there, a certainty came to him. After he cleared his name, he was going to resign. There was a woman he wanted to see—just one more time, before anonymity claimed him again.

Angrily, he turned away from the view and stalked into the house, shutting and locking the door behind him, then moved through the rooms without turning on the lights, confident of his path and of the decisions he'd just made.

There was another sort of darkness where Jeff was being held; a choking blackness where, at times, the air seemed too thick to breathe. At first, he'd been afraid that he would eventually die from lack of oxygen, and then he had remembered the breathing tube he'd seen in the ceiling. As the hours passed, he also discovered that daylight, although infinitesimal, was visible through the tiny tube and the knowledge, somehow, gave him peace.

He moved within the small enclosure, feeling his way from cot to table, fumbling his way through the packets of food, carefully sipping the water for fear this was all they would give him. Periodically, he would find his way to the steps, then go up them on his hands and knees until he got to the door, pushing hard with his hands and with his back, just on the off-chance someone had gotten careless and left it unlocked. But it was never so. Oddly enough, just the act of trying was enough to keep his spirits up—that and the hope that East would find him.

Ally raked a brush through her hair and then tossed it aside as she picked up a tube of lipstick, giving her lips a quick swipe. Her jeans were old but comfortable. Her pink and yellow, tie-dyed tank top was an alarming conglomeration of swirls and blobs, but she loved it. It was a rare concession to her youth, rather than to the austerity of her position with SPEAR.

In the other room, she could hear snatches of East's conversation with Foster Martin as he checked in with his second-in-command, making sure that all was going well at the resort. As she exited the bathroom, she looked toward the bed, trying to remember where she'd left her shoes, but they were nowhere in sight. She headed toward the living room, gathering up a file of papers as she went, anxious to get down to work.

East had already spoken with the chief of staff at the hospital where Jeff worked. Ally didn't know exactly what had been said, but she knew that East had made sure Jeff would not be penalized for missing school or work when he returned. It was a tricky situation, making certain that no one reported Jeff Kirby missing, because the last thing they needed or wanted was for the police to become involved in the search. It would drive Jeff's kidnappers even further underground and possibly anger Jonah's enemy to the point of having Jeff killed.

She entered the living room, put down her file and began looking for her shoes. East turned and waved, then quickly brought his phone call to an end. As soon as he hung up, he turned to Ally.

"What are you doing?" he asked.

"Looking for my shoes."

"They're in the kitchen under the table."

"Oh! Right! I kicked them off while I was working last night. Thanks."

She headed toward the kitchen, leaving East with a delightful view of her backside.

He shook his head, then swiped a hand over his face, as if wiping out the thoughts that kept going through his mind. It was very out of character for him, but he was having the devil of a time keeping his hands off of her.

"Found 'em," she yelled, then added a few moments later. "Want some breakfast?"

"Yes," he said. "But there's nothing here to cook. We're either going to have to shop for groceries or have food delivered."

Ally appeared in the doorway, a frown on her face. "Do they deliver breakfast?"

He shrugged. "Hell if I know. It's L.A., so probably. However, let's go find a store, buy some food for later and I'll treat you to breakfast before we get down to work."

She looked back at the microscope and the slides. "Maybe I should—"

East took her by the hand. "Look, nobody wants my son found worse than I do, but you have to eat. We won't be gone long. Besides, you said you needed a modem to hook up to your laptop."

"Oh, that's right, I do," she said. "Okay, let's go."

Just as they opened the door, a couple exited the elevator down the hall and started toward them.

"Oh, you must be our new neighbors," the woman said, offering her hand. "We're Mil and Bill. Mil is short for Millie, you know, but I like Mil better. Millie is so bourgeois."

Before East could comment, she let forth with a second burst of chatter.

"I told Bill the other night that it was too bad that nice young man was moving because he was such a good neighbor." She giggled. "Of course, part of the reason he was so good was because he was rarely here. He was a medical student, I believe. Anyway, do you and your wife have children? Bill and I don't. Not that I'm against the idea, but parenting is such a confining life-style, don't you agree?"

Ally wanted to take a deep breath for the woman because she didn't seem able to slow down long enough to breathe for herself. However, the woman had volunteered one useful bit of information, and East wasted no time in questioning her about it.

"Why did you think that Jeff had moved?" he asked.

Bill started to answer, but Mil jumped in ahead of him. "You knew him?" She rolled her eyes, then giggled. "Of course you must have, you just called him by name."

Finally, Bill interrupted. "You're Jeff's father, aren't you? I think we were introduced a year or so ago."

East nodded. "Yes, but back to my question. Why did you think Jeff had moved?"

"Oh! I remember you now. Sorry, I feel so silly, but when we came back from the hospital that night… Oh, that was just awful," Millie said, flying off in another conversational direction. "Someone called us a few nights ago…the night we saw the movers…and told us we needed to go to a hospital to identify my mother's body. Why I nearly died myself. We left immediately, of course, but the most awful thing…well, it wasn't really awful, because she wasn't there after all, and when we realized it was a hoax, we were really glad. Anyway, someone lied to us just to get us out of our apartment, Bill said. We raced home, certain that we'd come back to find we'd been robbed. Imagine our relief when everything was all right."

East glanced at Ally, but it was obvious by the look on her face that she was already on the same wavelength as him.

"So, why did you think Jeff was moving?" he repeated.

"Why…because of those three men in coveralls. They came out of your son's apartment carrying a great big trunk and after that, we didn't see him anymore so we just assumed that he had moved."

"What did they look like?" East asked.

Bill shrugged. "I didn't pay any attention."

"Oh, you know," Mil said. "Ordinary white men. One was a little taller and older than the other two and they were all wearing blue coveralls and baseball caps. Why, is something wrong?" She suddenly clapped her hands against her cheeks. "Oh, my! Was Jeff robbed instead of us? Why I never thought of that, did you, Bill?''

"No, no," East said quickly. "He wasn't robbed."

"Oh, that must have been the stuff he was shipping to you for storage," Ally said, giving East the alibi he needed to put this couple off the idea that anything was wrong.

"Right," East said.

"So Jeff hasn't moved?" Bill asked.

East shook his head. "No. He's on some sort of trade-out with a hospital in another state...specialized trauma work, or something of the sort."

The couple nodded. "Hope he does well," Bill said, and then added. "Nice to see you again."

It was all East could do to stay quiet until they were gone.

"God all mighty," he whispered. "I'd lay odds that Jeff was in that trunk and those men carried him out right under their noses."

Ally nodded. "Okay, now we know there were three men, and they had a big trunk, so it's doubtful that they were in a car or even a pickup truck. They would want some kind of an enclosed vehicle to move him away, and I'm betting on a van, although they could have had some sort of a rental truck."

"After we get back from breakfast, I'm going to question some of the people who live here. Maybe someone saw something that night that could help us."

"And maybe I'll find something in those fingerprints I lifted," Ally said. Impulsively, she gave East a quick hug. "This is wonderful," she said. "See...already we have hope because we have new clues. We'll find him, East. I just know it."

East smiled ruefully. "Where were you ten years ago? I could have used your faith and optimism then."

"Umm, I believe I was still wearing braces and working on my first Ph.D...or was it my second?"

"My God," East muttered. "I keep forgetting how young you are."

She pursed her lips in a rather puritan mode and gave him a disgusted look.

"Age is nothing but a state of mind. Personally, I can't remember a day of youthful exuberance in my entire life. I think I've always been old."

This time, it was East who reached out, pulling her close against his chest.

"I'm going to make you a promise, Ally girl. When this is over, I'm going to teach you something you don't know."

"What's that?" she asked.

"I'm going to teach you how to play."

It was late afternoon and the evening sun was coming through the kitchen window with bright persistence. Squinting against the glare, Ally shoved her chair back from the table and strode to the window, turning the slats on the shade until the room was bathed in a warm, homey glow. She tilted her head to the right, then to the left, wincing in satisfaction as her neck suddenly popped. Then she sat back down, pulled her laptop forward and resumed what she'd been doing.

It had been simple, hacking into the database at FBI headquarters. It wasn't the first time she'd done it, but never had the act been as personal to her as it was now.

During her forensic investigation, she'd found several different fingerprints, which stood to reason, since East claimed that Jeff occasionally entertained some of his med-school buddies. And, she'd identified Jeff's and one other young man's right off. But it was the partial she'd found on a large shard of glass that interested her most. She had every chance to expect that the print could very easily have come from the man who'd cleaned up the broken glass. All she had to do was wait while the program ran, hoping she would get a match.

The blood she'd typed had been the same type as Jeff's, which virtually eliminated the possibility of linking it to someone else. Because of that, they had little else to go on, save the print. If that bombed, it left them with nothing but vague descriptions of three white men in blue coveralls. Now, she sat staring at the screen as, one after the other, it sorted through the thousands of prints on file, looking for the one with the same set of whorls and indentations as the print she'd found on the glass.

A short while later, she glanced at her watch, then got up again, this time moving toward the living room and the terrace beyond. East had gone out some time ago, intent on talking to some of the other tenants to see if they'd noticed any unusual activity the night Jeff disappeared. The file Jonah had sent him was spread out on the coffee table, and although East had remarked upon the thoroughness employed by the man who was trying to take Jonah down, he hadn't been able to find anything pertinent that might help them find Jeff.

She opened the patio door and walked out on the small, balconied terrace, then sat down to watch the comings and goings from the parking lot below. So many people, and yet no one had noticed a young man had gone missing within their midst. Within their worlds, it was as if Jeff Kirby had never existed. Yet

Ally knew that he had. She'd seen pictures of him and East together—both men laughing into the camera's eye at some lost bit of nonsense: Jeff holding up a huge big-mouthed bass caught while on a Colorado fishing trip, East flipping hamburgers on an outdoor grill.

Ally sighed. East and Jeff had packed more "family" stuff into the last ten years they'd been together than she and her parents had done in her entire life. In fact, she couldn't remember a single time when her parents had gone out of their way to make her feel important. They'd left the discovery of that issue up to Ally, herself.

She kicked back in the chair and then closed her eyes, wanting so badly to give that life back to East. Mentally, she began reviewing the true facts of Jeff's disappearance, as she knew them.

There was the cryptic message from Jeff about walking away from a crash and burn.

The name Bob, written in blood on the floor of Jeff's apartment.

The three men who'd been seen carrying a trunk out of his apartment.

The so-far, unidentified fingerprint she'd found on the glass.

She opened her eyes and sat up, frustrated that they didn't know more. Again, she glanced at her watch. Almost an hour had passed since she'd come outside and she began to wonder what had happened to East. Hope began to rise as the sun began to set. Maybe he was on to something important—something that would set them on the right path to finding his son.

She stood abruptly, suddenly anxious to check on the program that was running. Maybe a match had been made.

As she started to leave, a flash of silver caught the corner of her eye and she turned back to the parking lot, curious as to what it was that she'd seen. When she saw nothing, she shrugged, and turned again, and again, the same flash of brilliance occurred. This time she stood, looking at the light from the corner of her eye until she'd focused on the exact location.

As she turned, she realized she had been looking at something affixed to a pole in the bank parking lot across the street. When she realized what it was, her heart skipped a beat. It was one of a couple of visible security cameras. But the implications of that particular camera were impossible to ignore. Unless she was mistaken, the background images of that particular camera would most likely be the vehicles going in and out of Jeff's apartment complex.

Her first impulse was to dash across the street, flash her government badge and demand to see the tapes. But then she remembered the time and realized that the establishment had probably been closed for quite a while. It would have to wait until tomorrow.

Excited about a possible new lead, she hurried back inside, hopeful that by now the fingerprint program had found a match. To her frustration, it was still running. Shrugging off the disappointment, she began rummaging through the refrigerator for something to fix for their dinner. She was debating between the two steaks East had bought or pasta and salad when she heard the front door open. Anxious to tell him her new theory, she dumped the stuff back in the fridge and bolted for the living room.

As East exited the elevator, he was surprised by a feeling of anticipation. Not since he was a kid had he experienced a sense of excitement at coming home. But today, he found himself hurrying down the hall toward Jeff's apartment. It was a little scary to accept the fact that it was Ally to whom he was hurrying. He couldn't help thinking that this attraction he was feeling couldn't have come at a more inopportune time, but he knew that matters of the heart were not things to be scheduled. All he could do was face the truth of his feelings and try not to let them get out of hand. Yet the more time he spent in her company, the more difficult that was beginning to be.

The key was in his hand, yet when he reached the door he hesitated, putting on what Jeff would have called his game face. Then he walked inside and she was coming toward him on the run and all of his good intentions evaporated. He slammed the door shut and caught her in midair.

"A man could get used to this kind of welcome," he drawled, and kissed her soundly before he could talk himself out of it.

The kiss was sweet, and from the gasp that he heard just before they connected, obviously unexpected. But it wasn't kissing her that bothered him. It was stopping at just the one.

Ally moaned, then leaned into him, her news momentarily forgotten. When he turned her loose, she staggered, and would have bumped into the sofa had he not grabbed her first.

She could feel her cheeks getting pink, but she refused to let him know how deeply it had affected her.

"That wasn't bad," she muttered. "Want to go out and come back in again…just to see if it could get any better?"

He laughed aloud and then hugged her again, but this time it was nothing more than a friendly embrace.

"I think I'd better stop while I'm ahead," he said.

She pretended to pout. "I was afraid you'd say that." Then the moment passed as she remembered why she'd been running to meet him. "Come with me," she said, grabbing him by the hand and pulling out to the terrace. "There's something I want you to see."

He followed willingly, more than a little enchanted with the flirt she was becoming.

"So, what's the big deal?" he asked, as she pulled him to the railing, then stopped.

She waved her hand toward the street. "Look out there. What do you see?"

East looked and saw nothing but cars and people and endless tons of cement.

"Don't I get a hint?" he asked.

Her eyebrows knotted momentarily, and then she grinned and pointed. "Smile. You're on candid camera."

He looked again, and in that moment, realized he was looking across the street and straight at a pole-mounted security camera. It didn't take more than a second for the implications to dawn, and when they did, he started to grin.

"Ally, honey, I said you were going to be my lucky charm."

She gave him an exasperated look. "And I told you I'm not lucky, I'm just—"

"Smart. Yeah, I know, you're smart. And thank the good Lord that you are."

"I wasn't going to say that," she argued. "I just pay attention to details." Then she frowned. "But we have to wait until tomorrow to get the tapes. I just hope to goodness they keep at least a week's worth before taping over them.''

But East wouldn't deny himself this new bit of hope.

''Grab your purse,'' he said. ''I'm taking you out for dinner.''

''But I was going to—''

''Do you want to cook?'' he asked.

She shrugged. ''I'm not very good at it.''

He grinned. ''Well, well, is there actually something you admit you don't know how to do?''

''Oh, no. I know *how* to cook, but I'm not good at it. That's one of those things where practice makes perfect, and there have been very few times, if any, that cooking has been a prerequisite for going undercover.''

He shook his head and then herded her back inside. ''Go do whatever it is that women do to make themselves happy to face the world, and hurry. Suddenly, I'm starving.''

''But the fingerprint ID is still running on my laptop.''

He took her by the shoulders, resisting the urge to shake her.

''And it will either be running when we get back, or it will have ended. Either way, there's nothing else we can do tonight.''

''Well, okay then,'' she said, and started toward the bedroom to change her clothes. By the time she reached the door, she was running.

Chapter 10

Ally was waiting as East came out of the bank with a stack of tapes. Flashing a United States government badge had been all it took to get an audience with the bank president. Without going into details, East had asked for the tapes by hinting that they might be valuable to an ongoing investigation. The president had jumped at the chance to cooperate and fifteen minutes later they were in East's hands, which moved him to the next step in his plans. There was a man from his past—a man named Freddie—who could work miracles with film. If there was anything to be seen on these tapes that would help them find Jeff, Freddie was the man who could find it.

"Where to now?" Ally asked.

"To visit an old friend," he said, as he scooted behind the steering wheel and dumped the tapes on the seat between them.

Forty-five minutes later, East had found the neighborhood and was now looking for a place to park.

"There's one," Ally said, pointing to an empty space in the middle of the block.

East whipped the car into the spot, then killed the engine. The neighborhood had changed, and from the amount of graffiti on the walls of the buildings, not for the better. He leaned forward, peering through the windshield to the building at the end of the block.

"From grocery store to video arcade," he muttered, eyeing the change of business below the second story of the building on the corner.

"What?" Ally asked.

"Nothing, just talking to myself," he said, then grabbed the videos. "Let's go see Freddie."

"How long has it been since you've seen him?" Ally asked.

"A little over ten years," East answered.

"How do you know he still lives here?"

"If he's still alive, he's here," East said, and opened the door.

Ally followed, slinging her purse over her shoulder as she stepped up on the curb. This place and its inhabitants could have been a clone of her last assignment. Tough places and tough people were nothing new to her, but she took comfort from the weight of the Luger in the bottom of her bag.

They entered the arcade to the mechanical sound of ringing bells and bionic beeps. Computerized roars and crashes sounded from the games that they passed, and the money the kids were feeding into the games seemed out of context in a neighborhood that appeared to have no signs of livelihood at all, save a liquor store across the street and a series of bars.

Ally walked with her hand on her bag, constantly aware that there were probably kids in this place who had killed, and who, for as little as fifty dollars, would do it again.

East moved carefully among the motley rank while keeping his eye on the archway at the end of the room. Once they moved through it to the dark hallway beyond, the noise was somewhat diminished.

"Here," he said, pointing to a series of steps leading up to the next story.

Ally moved in front of him and started up, thankful that East was at her back. Moments later, they reached the second-story landing. At East's instructions, she took a quick right.

"Good grief," she said, as they arrived at Freddie's door.

The paint on the black door was cracked and peeling, but there was no mistaking the white skull and cross-bones set dead center, nor the one word message, No, written below it.

"No, what?" Ally asked.

"No to everything," East answered.

Ally grinned. "A man of few words, I take it?"

"You have no idea," East said, and knocked.

Thirty seconds passed before East knocked again, and this time he made a fist, then pounded and yelled.

"Hey, Frederick Gene, are you home?"

Almost immediately, the door swung inward, revealing a tall, skinny man with a seventies Afro and a long, graying beard. His clothes were a reflection of his hair and the glare on his face lasted all of two seconds before he broke into a grin.

"By God, it's Easty boy! I thought you were dead!"

"Yeah, and I heard you downloaded a satellite feed

off a UFO and disappeared into thin air,'' East said, laughing as the man drew him into a thumping embrace.

''And wouldn't that be the ultimate trip?'' Freddie said, and pulled East into the room. Only then did he notice East wasn't alone. His smile stilled and his eyes narrowed. ''Who's the skirt?''

''I'm not wearing a skirt,'' Ally said shortly, ''and the name is Alicia Corbin.'' She held out her hand, as if daring him not to shake it.

''Go ahead,'' East said. ''She won't bite.'' Then in an aside to Ally, he explained. ''Freddie had a bad experience with a woman.''

''Yeah, man,'' Freddie said. ''She set her purse down on a keyboard and crashed the motherboard to one of my satellite feeds.''

''When did that happen?'' Ally asked.

Freddie squinted. ''About ten, maybe twelve years ago. I forget.''

''Holds a grudge, too,'' she muttered, glancing about the room at the array of computer equipment in the room behind him. Then her eyes widened and her mouth parted in a silent *O* as she walked past them in silent awe.

Ignoring a small jealous spurt that he hadn't been able to put that look on her face, East glanced at Freddie.

''I think she just fell in love.''

Freddie spun and hurried after her, afraid she would touch his stuff. But he need not have worried. Ally moved about the room, gazing at one setup, then another, and another, admiring them as a patron of the arts might enjoy the great masters while strolling about the Louvre. It took a couple of minutes before Freddie settled down, and only then did he ask why they'd come.

East held up the tapes. "I need help," he said.

"What's on them?" Freddie asked.

"I hope a clue as to who's got my son."

Freddie's eyes widened as he sucked his lower lip into his mouth. Without speaking, he dropped onto a backless stool and rolled toward a VCR, shoving in the first tape and hitting Play as the castors on his stool settled into little grooves on the old hardwood floor. Images appeared immediately.

"What are we looking for?" he asked.

"Three men in coveralls carrying a large trunk. I'm not sure what they're driving…maybe a van or a rental truck."

Freddie nodded and slid a pair of Ben Franklin style eyeglasses up the bridge of his nose then leaned forward.

"The kid…Jeff…is he all right?"

East sighed. "He was day before yesterday."

Freddie glanced up once. "Grudge?" he asked, indicating that he knew more about East's past than Ally would have imagined.

"Same as," East said, then glanced at Ally, seeing the question in her eyes. "Freddie trained me."

It all became clear. Freddie was a retired SPEAR operative, which explained everything else. East's willingness to trust him with information, the odd lifestyle, the skull and crossbones on his door, his distrust of people and his unusual expertise.

Silence filled the room as three pairs of eyes became trained upon the black-and-white images moving on the screen. Occasional noise from the arcade below was distracting, but as time passed, they subconsciously blocked it out, much in the same way that Freddie had learned to do.

An hour passed, then another, and another. That tape played out and they inserted a second. A couple more minutes played out and then suddenly East pointed.

"That's Jeff's car."

They watched the four-wheel drive sports utility move through the apartment gates and then come to a stop near the front entrance. A vague image of a man exited and East found himself blinking back tears.

Damn, damn, damn. Don't let this be the last sight I ever have of my son.

"Is that him?" Ally asked.

East nodded as the man disappeared off-screen.

Nothing else appeared on the tape that seemed pertinent. East's nerves were on edge as Freddie slid in the last one. He'd been so confident when the day had started, and now this one was their last hope. Daylight became dark on the tape and the parking lot emptied. Despite the thirty-five mile an hour speed limit in front of the apartment building, traffic moved at a swift pace.

Suddenly Ally gasped and pointed to the right of the screen.

"There! A dark van pulling into the apartment complex!"

Freddie started to hit rewind when East touched his shoulder. "Wait," he said. "Let it play. We can always go back."

As the van turned, it moved out of camera range and East groaned, then moments later, appeared at the right of the screen again.

"Son of a...look where they parked," East said.

Ally and Freddie peered closer. The van had parked beneath a broken street light.

"Odd choice of parking place when there are plenty of vacancies in better lighting," East muttered.

"They aren't getting out," Ally said.

East's heart skipped a beat. She was right. Something told him they were about to get lucky.

"Watch the van," he said sharply.

Within minutes, both doors opened simultaneously and three men spilled out into the shadows. Two of them were carrying something large between them, but there was no way they could get a look at their faces.

"Well, hell," East said, as the trio went in the front of the apartment. All they could see were their backs and the trunk they were carrying.

"Maybe we'll get them when they come out," Freddie said.

Instinctively, Ally moved closer to East, offering comfort in the only way that she could—by her presence.

Minutes passed—long agonizing minutes of watching cars and traffic, all the while knowing that while that camera was rolling, Jeff was most likely fighting for his life.

Suddenly, Freddie pointed. "There they come!"

Again, the trio's faces were hidden by shadows and the angle of their heads, but there was no mistaking the trunk they were carrying, or the fact that it was taking all three of them to carry it now. They moved out of camera range, appearing seconds later on the dark side of the van.

"Stop tape," East said. "Now, can you zoom in on that shot?"

"Yeah, but I don't think we're gonna see anything," Freddie said, and punched a couple of keys on his keyboard.

Immediately, the picture enlarged, then enlarged again. Freddie hit a couple more keys then moved the cursor to a specific section of the picture and clicked. At once, a specific section of the picture was separated from the whole, which he enlarged, then enlarged again.

"Can't go any higher," Freddie said. "I'm already losing clarity and density."

"Print it out," East said.

Freddie clicked the mouse and a printer to Ally's left kicked on. Seconds later, it spit out a print. She handed it to East. The men's faces were indistinct blobs of dark and light.

"Damn it," East muttered. "Play out the rest of the tape."

They watched as the van backed up, then disappeared from view, appearing seconds later as it exited the gate. As it turned into the traffic, they had a brief glimpse of a license plate before another car drove up beside the van, blocking it from the camera's view.

"Back it up," East said.

Freddie hit Rewind.

"There!" East said, pointing to the small, indistinct rectangle on the back of the van. Can you blow up that tag?"

Freddie grinned. "Do bears…"

Ally interrupted, laughing. "I think that's a yes."

A few clicks later, they had a printout of the van's tag as well. Freddie handed it to East with a flourish, then pointed to a nearby drawer.

"There's a magnifying glass in there," he said.

Ally hurried toward it, returning with the large, round glass.

"Here," she said, thrusting it into East's hand.

He leaned forward, holding it over the pictures that he'd laid beneath the light.

"I can't make out all of the numbers, but I can make out the state."

"Idaho or New York?" Ally asked.

East straightened abruptly, his eyes round with shock.

"How did you know?"

"Crash and burn, remember?"

"Son of a bitch," he mumbled, and lifted the magnifying glass to his face one more time, reassuring himself that what he'd seen was truly there. Then he handed the glass to Ally.

"You tell me," he said.

She leaned down. When she straightened, she was smiling.

"Yippee-kiyi-yay, cowboy, it's Idaho, just like your son called it."

"He told you?" Freddie asked.

"Not exactly," East said. "It's a long story." Then he combed his fingers through his hair in frustration. "My God…if this is so…if his kidnappers have actually taken him to Idaho, how in hell do we find him?" Then he slapped the flat of his hand on the desk in frustration. "Do you know how big the state of Idaho is?"

"Actually, yes," Ally said. "It's 83,557 square miles, including eight hundred and eighty square miles of inland water. It's thirteenth in size among the fifty states and its highest elevation is Borah Peak, which is 12,662 feet above sea level."

Freddie gawked. "What is she, a walking encyclopedia?"

Ally looked crestfallen. She'd blurted out the answer

before she'd thought. But to her delight, East just grinned, and ruffled her hair.

"Nope. She's my lucky charm."

His words took the sting out of Freddie's thoughtless remark, although she would have preferred something more from East than a pat on the head.

"I just know stuff," Ally said, and pretended great interest in the pictures they'd printed out.

Freddie began to smile. "You know, if my last girl-friend had been half as smart as I suspect you are, we might still be warming the sheets." He winked at East and turned toward Ally, leaning back on his stool and folding his arms across his chest. "Say, if you get tired of old Easty boy, you come on back here. I've got all kinds of toys for you to play with."

Ally laughed out loud. From anyone else, the rude, sexual innuendo would have been insulting. But coming from this tall, skinny reject from the seventies, it was comical, and they all knew it.

Freddie pretended to frown. "Am I to take that as a refusal?"

"Pretty much," Ally said, "although I have to say it's the best offer I've had all day."

Freddie pursed his lips and tugged on his beard as he swiveled the stool around to stare at East.

"What's the matter with you, Easty boy? Looks like your son isn't the only thing you've lost. I can remember the days when you would have—"

"Butt out," East muttered, as Ally glanced at her watch.

"The program," she said. "It has to be finished by now. Maybe we got lucky there, too."

"What program?" Freddie asked.

"I'm running a match on a fingerprint we found in Jeff's apartment."

Freddie's eyes rounded and then squinted as a wide grin began to spread.

"You hacked into the FBI system to run a print?"

Ally pursed her lips. "I didn't exactly hack," she said. "I have clearance, you know."

He grinned. "Yeah, but not from a civilian PC. I'm impressed."

She smiled primly.

East sighed and then grinned. "You're right, honey. One step at a time." He glanced at Freddie. "Old friend, you don't know what this means to me."

Freddie's smile faded. "Oh, I think I do." He hesitated, thoughtfully eyeing Ally, then added. "You're both going to Idaho, aren't you?"

East nodded.

Freddie stood abruptly and strode to a nearby cabinet, took something from a shelf, and then handed it to East.

"What's this for?" East asked, eyeing the set of keys Freddie had put in his hand.

"*Baby.* She's in storage, but I was just there last week and everything is operative, including a new battery under the hood."

"*Baby?* Who's *Baby?*" Ally asked.

"You'd have to see her to believe her," East said, then looked at Freddie. "Are you sure you want to do this?"

Freddie squinted, as if unwilling to show the emotion welling in his eyes. "Well, yes. Wouldn't have offered, otherwise. Besides, you got to get that kid back and get him through the rest of his school. Never know when I might need some free doctoring."

East clasped the key tight in his fist, then cleared his throat. "We'll take good care of her."

"It's the kid that matters most," Freddie said. "You just find him."

The two men embraced briefly then stepped apart. Freddie winked at Ally as they started to leave. "I'd give you a hug, too, except I don't think old Easty boy would appreciate my generosity."

"I field my own hugs," Ally said.

Freddie laughed and swooped.

Ally found herself momentarily nose to beard, felt a swift kiss on her forehead and then was set aside as abruptly as she'd been held. A little embarrassed, she smoothed at the front of her blouse and then patted her hair.

"Thank you," she said, primly.

Freddie laughed again. "You're welcome." Then he looked at East, who was trying not to frown. "Man, you're done for and you don't even know it."

They could still hear him laughing as he shut the door behind them. The sound of voices and videos drifted up the stairwell, mixing with the dust and gloom in which they were standing. East gave Ally a long, slow look.

"Am I?" he suddenly asked.

Her eyebrows knitted. "Are you what?"

"Done for?"

Her eyes widened, then focused on his mouth before she abruptly looked away.

"I don't know what you're talking about," she muttered. "Let's get back to the apartment. I have a good feeling about that print."

He followed her down the stairs and through the ar-cade, watching the sway of her hips as she strode purposefully through the crowd—so certain of her skill and intelligence, and yet so unsure of herself as a woman. Never in his life had he been more confused, or as certain that he was falling in love.

"We've got a match!" Ally shouted.

East dropped the keys onto the table and ran toward the kitchen.

Ally had dashed through the door the moment he'd unlocked it, bolting ahead of him to see if the program she'd been running was finished. From the tone of her voice, it was good news.

"Please tell me it's not one of his friends," East muttered, as he leaned over her shoulder to look at the screen.

Ally shook her head. "Not unless he's running with a crowd you don't know about." She pointed. "Elmore Todd. White male, forty-six years old, two hundred and thirty-four pounds, six feet two inches tall. Priors— assault and battery, armed robbery. Sentenced five to ten, served two and a half years in Soledad, released in 1988. Picked up for possession of an illegal weapon in 1993, but the charges were dismissed."

She kept scrolling the information, reading the arrests and dispensations without comment until she came to the bottom of the page. Suddenly, she gasped. "East! Look at this!"

He leaned closer, reading where she was pointing.

"Born in New Township, Idaho. Ties to three known militia groups within the state—America's Freemen, Sons of Glory, and the Brotherhood of Blood."

"Son of a bitch," East muttered, trying not to think of what people like that might do to his son. "But why them? What would a militia group have to do with trying to bring down a man like Jonah? Their agenda is usually broader than that.''

''You've been out of the loop too long,'' Ally said. ''It's well known within SPEAR that some of those groups are little more than mercenaries, willing to hire out to the highest bidder.''

East stood abruptly. ''That fits in with my theory that the man who wants Jonah is not in the same place as the people who took Jeff. If you're right…if he hired some right-wing militia group to snatch Jeff, then we're in big trouble, aren't we?''

She shook her head, disinclined to admit she was scared. ''Maybe not, although there are so many off-shoots of known, organized groups that it may be very difficult to find the one that this man is connected with now.'' Then she added. ''But not impossible.''

''I've got to talk to Jonah,'' East said. ''The kidnapper is going to call soon and when he does, I'm going to need some bargaining power.''

''You're going to give the kidnapper real info?'' she asked.

''No, but it's going to look that way. By the time he figures it out, I have to have Jeff safely in my possession.''

''That's risky. What if we don't find him before—''

''We'll find him,'' East said. ''We have no choice.'' Then he pulled Ally out of the chair and grasped her by the shoulders. ''I said you were my lucky charm, and I meant it. It would have taken me days, even weeks to get this much information by myself.'' Then he added. ''Hell, I don't even know if I would ever have gotten this far. You're right, I've been out of the loop too long.''

''Actually, your instincts are still there, and you've

got one thing going for you that neither Jonah or the kidnappers have.''

''What's that?'' he asked.

''Your love for Jeff. A parent's love for a child is stronger than any force on earth.'' Then she sighed and her voice dropped. ''At least it should be.''

East pulled her into his arms and held her close. ''I wish I could change the way you were raised. There are people who should never have children, and even though your childhood was not ideal, I'm really glad you were born.''

She smiled against the fabric of his shirt and closed her eyes, fighting back tears.

''Me, too,'' she said. ''And I'll do everything I can to help you find Jeff.''

He lifted her chin until their gazes met. His eyes were dark with warning.

''I'll take your help and gladly,'' he said. ''But when this is over, prepare yourself, because I'm going to ask something more of you than just help.''

She shivered suddenly, uncertain of what to say. Then he was coming closer, blocking out her vision of everything except the want in his eyes.

Mouths merged, opening gently to the pressure, tasting the sweetness of trust and the beginnings of love.

Chapter 11

Night came to L.A. It had been eleven days since Ally had appeared at Condor Mountain, and four days since the phone call about Jeff's disappearance. East's stomach clenched. Time was running out. Tomorrow they would retrieve Freddie's *Baby* and head for Idaho. After that, the plan was vague. All he could do was hope that the threads of this mess would keep unraveling as they went, because staying stationary was no longer an option.

East came out of the bathroom wearing a pair of sweatpants and nothing else. His hair was still damp and spiky from his shower and his bare feet made soft splatting sounds as he came down the hall, intent on telling Ally that the bathroom was free. He rounded the corner with her name on his lips and ran squarely into her. She staggered backward as the stack of papers she was carrying went flying.

"Ally, honey! I'm so sorry. Are you all right?"

She rolled her eyes and pressed a hand to her midriff. "Except for the fact that you scared me senseless, I'm fine." Then she dropped to her knees and began to gather up the papers.

East knelt beside her. "Let me do that. It's my fault they fell."

"No, I'm perfectly capable of—"

He grabbed her hand, then tugged. "Ally, look at me."

She looked up, a slight flush on her face.

"I know what you're capable of, probably better than you do," he said gently. "Now go take your bath and relax. I will pick up the damned papers. Do you understand?"

Her lips pursed.

"Aren't you going to tell me to go to hell?" he teased, trying to make her smile.

She stood abruptly. "Why should I tell you something that you seem perfectly capable of figuring out for yourself?" she said, and stepped around him, striding down the hall with her head held high.

He rocked back on his heels and started to laugh.

"One of these days, Ally, girl. One of these days," he called out.

The bathroom door slammed shut.

He was still chuckling as he gathered the last of her papers and put them on the dining room table, then stood in the quiet until he heard water running in the bathroom down the hall. Only then did he move to the terrace. As he did, he was surprised to feel moisture on his face. He hadn't even known it was raining. He stood for a moment in the shadows, taking shelter from the shallow overhang and listened to the sounds.

Raindrops peppered upon metal surfaces like the tinkling sounds of a player piano, clinking, dripping, running, pouring. Water fell in gushes from the downspouts onto the concrete below, mini-cascades that ran fast and free. He leaned against the wall and crossed his arms over his chest, relishing the fresh breeze and mist upon his bare arms and chest. Then he closed his eyes, wondering if it was raining where Jeff was being held—worrying if he was cold—afraid he might be hungry. Ah God, he couldn't face losing Jeff and live knowing that again, the death of an innocent would be on his shoulders; and this time his own son.

Time passed. He never knew when the rain stopped, or that Ally had been standing in the shadows of the living room for quite some time, watching the changing expressions on his face. All he knew was for the first time in years, he was scared.

He shivered, but was reluctant to go to bed and face the ghosts of his past. Finally the chill of the night got to him and he pushed away from the wall and turned to go inside when he saw Ally.

She was standing in the dark wearing that same oversize T-shirt with her hands clasped at her waist as if she was about to recite a lesson. But it was the expression on her face that stopped him flat.

Sweet heaven, hadn't anyone ever told that woman not to let a man see her vulnerability? He frowned, then moved inside, closing and locking the patio door behind him.

''It got cold.''

She swallowed, trying to find something insignificant to talk about, but when he looked at her like that, she couldn't think.

''Want something to drink?'' he asked, and took a step toward her.

She flinched, then shook her head.

He had to give it to her—she had guts. She looked scared to death and yet held her ground. His sigh deepened. This had to stop. If they were going to find Jeff, they had to work together, and not just during the day when there were clues to unravel, but all the time. Trust was a twenty-four hour emotion or it wasn't there at all.

"Are you afraid of me?"

She hesitated, and it stunned him to realize how much that hurt.

"Damn it, Alicia, I would never force you into anything you don't want. Don't you know that?"

It was the pain in his voice that made her find her own.

"I'm sorry, I'm sorry," she said quickly. "It's not that. It's not even you." She lowered her head. "It's me."

He moved toward her, touching her face, then tilting her chin and forcing her to look at him when she talked.

"What about you?" he asked.

"I don't know how to handle all of this."

His voice softened. "All of what, honey?"

"You. Me. Us."

He smiled gently. "Is there an us?"

She blushed. "See. That's what I mean. I don't know. I can't read the signs. I don't know the rules. All I know is when we get like this it's hard to catch my breath. Is that just lust, or is it something else?"

Her naivete and honesty shamed him. It was time he stopped pushing her. He took her hand, then pulled her closer.

"I don't know how you feel. I can only tell you how I feel about us, okay?"

"Okay."

Her eyes were wide and fixed upon his face, and then he took her into his arms, burying his face in the soft curls at the crown of her head.

"I see your smile in my dreams. Hearing you laugh makes my stomach knot, and the trust in your eyes makes me humble. At any odd moment of the day, I wonder what it would be like to make love to you, and I don't want to think of the day we say goodbye."

"Oh, East," Ally whispered, then pulled away from his embrace and covered her face with her hands.

East's heart dropped, but he tried to make light of his disappointment.

"Dang, honey, is making love to me that hard to face?"

She shuddered, then looked up. "It's not that. Oh no, it's never that."

"Then what?"

She took a deep breath. "I've never made love. I don't know how." And before East could comment, she added. "Oh, I've read books. Lots of books. But something tells me that there's a lot more to it than the act itself."

East was stunned, and yet when he thought about it, realized he should not have been. Struggling to find the right words that wouldn't make all this worse, he smiled and cupped the side of her face.

"As always, honey girl, you're right on the money. There's a lot more to making love than the act itself. But being an expert doesn't matter. In fact, saving yourself is something to be proud of. The man you marry is going to get quite a prize when he gets you."

A slight frown appeared between her eyebrows as she considered his words. "I don't know. Do you think that maybe, when this is all over of course…that you might show me?"

East felt as if someone had just punched him in the belly.

"Show you?"

Her frown deepened. "Yes, you know…show me how to make love?"

"But I just said that being a virgin for the man you marry is a special—"

"I know all of that," she said shortly. "But I've found that experience is preferable to fumbling folly."

"Fumbling folly."

She sighed. If he kept repeating everything she said, they would get nowhere.

"Ineptitude then, if you prefer."

He started to grin. "I think I prefer."

Her eyes brightened. "Oh! Well then, is it a deal?"

He nodded. "Oh yeah, it's a deal."

She pursed her lips slightly as she considered his pledge, then folded her hands in front of her in that funny little way and smiled.

"I believe I'll go to bed now," she said, then added, "If that's all right with you."

He nodded again, all but speechless.

"Okay then," Ally said, suddenly unsure of this silent behavior. "Uh…good night."

East found his voice enough to answer. "Yes, good night."

She stood uncertainly for another moment, then finally left the room.

As East watched her go, his love went with her. She didn't know it yet, but right in the middle of her crazy reasoning, he'd fallen the rest of the way in love. Somehow, someway, he was going to make it all work between them, because there was no way in hell he was letting another man touch her.

The storage lot where Freddie kept *Baby* was huge; row after row of bunker-like buildings with identical doors and locks. The only difference between any of them were the numbers above the door.

"What number are we looking for?" Ally asked.

"Two hundred and twenty-eight."

Ally peered out the window to the nearest numbered building and rolled her eyes.

"This is stupid," she muttered.

"What's stupid?" East asked.

"They've built the entrance at the back of the lot. This is number 1420. That means we need to go south." She pointed toward the other end of the lot, past the endless stream of chain-link fence.

"South it is," East said, and accelerated slowly.

A short while later, he stopped, then turned down an aisle between the buildings and began looking for two hundred and twenty-eight.

"There it is," Ally said. "Third one down on your left."

"Leave it up to Freddie to find the cheapest method of long-term parking in L.A.," he said.

Within minutes, they had unlocked the overhead door and began pushing it up. It rolled on noisy brackets like a car driving over an old wooden bridge. East turned on the interior light, but it wasn't really necessary since the vehicle inside took up all but a narrow walking space on either side.

"Good grief," Ally said. "We aren't really going to drive this anywhere, are we?"

East had seen it before, but he still winced, picturing himself behind the wheel. The metal panels of the RV were a psychedelic swirl of greens, pinks and blues. It looked like an old whorehouse on wheels.

"Don't let me forget my sunglasses," he muttered, as he moved toward the ancient vehicle.

Ally snorted. "You aren't worried about harmful UV rays. You're just afraid someone you know will see you in this."

He laughed. "You may be right. However, wait until you see what's inside." He opened the door and then stood aside, letting her go in first. "There's a light switch to the left as you step up."

"It better be good, or—" She forgot what she'd been going to say. "Oh…my…God."

East had to push her gently to get her to move so that he could follow. Even then, Ally stood with her mouth agape, unable to believe her eyes at the array of state-of-the-art equipment inside.

"It's one of the best stake-out vehicles we ever used, and he has obviously updated it from time to time. Whatever you need is in here. Satellite feeds. Faxes. Computer systems, printers, video equipment, tracking devices…"

"Even telephone tracing systems," Ally added, running her fingers lightly over the console of one setup. Then she turned to East. "I am in heaven."

He poked the end of her nose with his forefinger and grinned.

"You just think this is heaven, honey. Wait until I expand your world and then tell me that again."

She frowned. "Expand my—?" She started to blush.

"Oh. You mean when we eventually make love that I will have a lesser appreciation for technical equipment?"

East's face was a study of momentary confusion, and then he burst out laughing. Before she could take offense, he hugged her close. "Honey, don't ever let anyone tell you that you aren't sexy, because you are. In fact, you're the most desirable woman I've ever met in my life."

Ally beamed. "Why, thank you. The feeling is mutual."

He shook his head and then handed her the keys to his car. "I'm going to drive this out. As soon as I do, pull my car inside. This is a perfect place to leave it."

Thirty minutes later, they had transferred their bags and supplies into *Baby* and were on their way.

Jeff woke abruptly into the airless dark, his heartbeat pounding like a sledgehammer against his eardrums, and for one second before sanity leveled, he thought he'd gone blind.

"Have mercy," he muttered, and rolled to a seated position on the edge of his cot.

He was cold. He'd been cold for so long. Despite the triple layer of blankets he'd been sleeping under, he hadn't been warm once since they'd put him in the hole. Wearily, he rubbed his hands over his face, scratching the heavy growth of whiskers. Never in his life had he wanted a shower and a shave as badly as he did now.

He stood carefully, feeling his way along the wall until he came to the edge of the table. Using his fingers to see, he felt for the cup he kept beside the water can. When he found it, his fingers carefully curled around the handle as he dipped it into the water. As he dipped, the cup suddenly scraped along the bottom in a tinny, rasping sound. He froze. That had never happened before. Bracing himself so that he wouldn't accidentally tip anything over, he put his other hand down in the can, feeling along the side for the level of water. To his dismay, he estimated less than three inches were left.

He hesitated, weighing his thirst against the possibility that these monsters would not respond to any more demands, and then poured the water in the cup back into the can and set it aside. He could wait a little longer to quench his thirst.

His stomach rumbled, but he'd already faced the dwindling supply of field rations and cut back on his food as well. He had no way of trusting that they would replenish what was here, and no way of knowing how long it would be before his father found him.

But the moment his father's face appeared in his mind's eye, he became even more determined to survive. God in heaven, it couldn't end like this. Life had kicked him in the teeth for fourteen years and then he'd met East. He still remembered the gut-wrenching fear of rounding a corner on that high mountain path and coming face-to-face with the man. But the darkness Jeff had seen in East's eyes had quickly turned to shock, then curiosity as they stood without speaking. It was East who'd finally broken the silence with a line that still made Jeff smile.

"Hey kid, aren't you kinda far out for pizza delivery?"

Jeff remembered grinning. It was a memorable occasion for many reasons, not the least of which was that he hadn't had anything to smile about in so long he thought he'd forgotten how.

He sighed, took four steps sideways then turned and began to pace.

Five steps forward.

Stop. Turn.

Five steps back.

Any more either way and he would hit wall.

He'd walked it so many times now that his count was subconscious, allowing him the freedom to pursue other thoughts. Periodically, he worried about his job and classes, wondering if they would let him back in, then reality would return. If East didn't find him, the concern was moot. And there were the times when a woman's face slipped through his mind. A woman with flashing brown eyes, dark, chin-length hair, who when she stretched, could look eye-to-eye with the second button down on his shirt.

His steps began to drag as the endless chill soaked deeper into his bones, yet he continued to move. Beads of sweat began to pearl on his forehead and upper lip, which when he thought about it, didn't compute. How in hell could he possibly sweat when he was cold all the way through?

Finally he stopped and looked up at the weak beam of pencil-thin light coming through the air tube. The hole was so small that the light rays seemed to disappear in midair halfway down to the floor. As he stood, something inside of him snapped, and he spun angrily and stomped toward the steps, bumping into his cot as he went. Halfway up, he tripped and fell, catching himself with outstretched hands, but not soon enough to save both knees from the impact. The pain only made his fury worse.

"Cowards! You're all a bunch of sorry cowards! I need water and some decent food. I need a bath and fresh air. Just because you people choose to live like animals, doesn't mean I will."

He hammered long and hard on the underside of the heavy metal door with his fists until they were numb and bleeding, and he still didn't stop. Finally, he gave the door a last angry blow, then moved down to the bottom of the stairs and then shouted at the top of his voice.

"You can kill me three ways to Sunday, but you won't break me. Do you hear me you bastards? You won't break me!"

Silence was his answer. With shaking steps, he made his way back to his cot and lay down. Pulling the blankets over his bruised and shaking body, he closed his eyes and escaped the only way he knew how—in his sleep.

It was night when East crossed the California border into Nevada. *Baby's* tires made a whining sound as they rolled along Interstate 15 into the desert stretching out before them. Ally rode silently in the passenger seat and he marveled at a woman who could be so silent for so long. The last time they'd traded words was when they'd stopped to eat, and now, her gaze stayed fixed upon the highway in front of them, as if she needed to keep watch just to keep them safe. He shook his head in silent wonder. If he'd had a partner like her before, he might not have come undone. Then he sighed. Before didn't matter. It was the hell they were in now that kept him simmering with unresolved anger.

"If you get tired, I'll drive," Ally said.

Her voice startled him, and it took him a moment to answer.

He thought of the wild colors on the outside of the vehicle and grinned. "Yeah, you wait until it's dark to get behind the wheel," he teased.

She smiled primly. "I'm no dummy."

He chuckled, then shook his head.

"Thanks, but I'm still good to go. However, when we get to the Prima Donna, I'm stopping for the night."

"Who's the Prima Donna?" she asked.

"It's not a who, it's a what," East said. "It's a casino about an hour or so west of Las Vegas."

She looked down at the map in her lap, squinting against the dim glow of the dashboard lights.

"I don't see any towns between here and there."

"There aren't."

She looked up. "You mean someone just built a casino in the middle of nowhere? Surely they don't get much business."

He shook his head. "Just wait and see."

She leaned her head against the seat, contemplating the wisdom of such folly, then settled back to wait as East said.

Sometime before midnight, Ally began to see a bright glow on the horizon. She shifted wearily in the seat and glanced at East, marveling that he showed no signs of the exhaustion she was feeling.

"We're almost there," he said.

She stood, and then walked back to the minuscule bathroom to wash her face and comb her hair. Not because she felt the need for grooming, but because she needed to do something to keep herself awake. When she came out, she took a soft drink out of the small bar-size refrigerator and carried it back to her seat. Popping the top, she took one long drink, then handed it to East without comment.

It occurred to him as he took it that, whether she knew it or not, she was becoming very comfortable with him and his presence. As he took a big drink, he wondered if she knew what she'd done; sharing the soft drink as she would with a friend.

He smiled in the dark, intrigued with the idea of her as a friend. He'd never made love to a very best friend, but something told him it was going to be special.

A short while later, he began to slow down. When he pulled into the parking lot of the Prima Donna Hotel and Casino, Ally was hanging out the window, staring in disbelief.

"They have a Ferris wheel," she muttered, pointing to the brightly lit sphere.

"Wait until you see what's inside."

Her eyes lit up. "What?"

"There's a merry-go-round on the ground floor for kids."

Her eyes widened. "They bring kids to places like this?"

"Oh honey, you have no idea."

She pointed across the highway to another large, brightly lit building. "Is that part of it, too?"

He shook his head. "No, but they share a tram of sorts."

"Amazing." Then she looked off to her right. "Look how many other people are parking here, too."

"No, those are trailer houses for the employees. We're too far out of Vegas for people to drive back and forth, so the owners just house their workers on the premises instead."

"Good grief," Ally exclaimed.

"It's an easy way to make sure that your employees show up on time."

A few minutes later, East pulled to a stop at the far edge of the parking lot.

"Now what?" Ally asked.

"We sleep. In the morning, I call Jonah. We're going to need some money, but he'll okay it. It wouldn't be the first time I had to pay for necessary information."

"What are you going to tell him?" she asked.

"As little as possible."

"When the kidnapper calls wanting information, what are you going to do?"

A muscle jerked in East's jaw. "Give it to him." Then he stood up, stretching his cramped muscles as he walked toward the back of the RV. "Are you hungry?"

"A little, but it's too late to eat. I think I'd rather sleep."

"Same here," East said. "You take the shower first, but remember, go easy on the water. We're not hooked up here, so we'll be using what's in store."

She nodded, then looked around, suddenly realizing that there were no beds in sight.

"Where do we sleep?" she asked.

"You'll see."

She shrugged, then went to clean up. A few minutes later she came out and almost stumbled on the two air mattresses in the middle of the floor. East was down on his knees, trying to put a contour sheet over the inflated pad.

"Bathroom's free. Let me," Ally said.

East stood, his cheeks red with frustration. "Have at

it,'' he muttered, grabbed his bag and disappeared into the tiny bathroom.

By the time he came out, Ally had claimed the mattress against the wall and was sound asleep, leaving the one closest to the door for him. He stood for a moment, watching the even rise and fall of her chest beneath the covers and felt an overwhelming surge of tenderness. Another woman might have made an issue of the fact that they would be sleeping in such close quarters, or possibly tried to jump his bones. But not Ally. They were partners, therefore she'd given him her trust. Yet when he lay down beside her, it was all he could do to focus on the gift when the woman he wanted was so near and dear. Certain that he would never be able to sleep, he closed his eyes. When he opened them, sunlight was shining in his face.

Chapter 12

Ally was gone. He raised up on one elbow and wiped the sleep from his eyes, and as he did, saw the note. He leaned across the mattress and picked it up, tilting it toward the light.

Went to get breakfast. Be back later.

Me

He tossed the note aside as he got up and dressed, then deflated the mattresses and packed them and the linens back in the cupboard beneath one of the computer consoles. After digging through the supplies they'd brought, he found Freddie's coffeemaker and started it up. The scent of freshly brewing coffee soon filled the enclosure, making his belly growl. He glanced out the window, wondering how long Ally had been gone, and debated with himself about going to look for her, but he couldn't really afford to leave. One

of them had to be by the phones at all times in case
Jonah—or the kidnapper—called again. Left with no
other options, he settled down to wait.

Half an hour passed and he was starting to get antsy
when he saw Ally coming across the parking lot carrying a rather large, brown paper bag. He opened the
door and waved. When she got closer, he called out to
her.

"What did you do, buy them out?"

She handed him the sack and then climbed inside.
"I didn't want to wake you."

"Something smells good," he said. "What's for
breakfast?"

"A little bit of everything, so sit. I'll serve."

"We don't have any dishes or cutlery. When we go
through Vegas, we need to get some disposable stuff."

"I know," she said. "I took care of the problem for
today."

He grinned. "Why am I not surprised."

She handed him a paper container and a large plastic
fork.

"Dig in."

He opened the lid, inhaling the food with appreciation as he forked a large bite of scrambled eggs and
sausage and popped it in his mouth.

"Umm," he said, chewing around the nonverbal
comment.

Ally smiled and opened her own, quickly digging in
to the food.

They ate in silence until both containers were empty,
then East picked them up and started to toss them in
the sack she'd been carrying.

"Wait!" she cried, and jumped up, stopping him
before he dropped the dirty stuff.

"What? I was going to use it for a trash container," East said.

She looked a little guilty, then took the sack and turned it upside down. Stacks of money fell out, some bundled in fives, a few in tens or twenties, the rest in one-hundred-dollar bills.

East gawked. "What the hell did you do?"

"Played a little blackjack."

He turned, staring at her in disbelief. "And you won…all this?"

"Well…yes."

"How long were you gone?"

She glanced at her watch. "Umm, about an hour I guess." Then she added. "But it took about fifteen minutes of that time to get the food."

East kept staring at the money. "So, what you're saying is you won all of that in forty-five minutes?"

"You said we needed some money to travel on."

"Yes, but…" He stopped and started over. "How did you do that?"

She smiled. "Oh, it's quite simple, actually. It's all a matter of remembering what's been played, then figuring the ratio of what cards are left in the shoe, then taking the average—"

"Never mind," he muttered, and sat down with a thump, staring at her in disbelief.

"Exactly how *much* money did you win…in forty-five minutes, of course."

"Five thousand, four hundred and fifty dollars. There was a hundred dollars more, but I read where it's acceptable to tip the dealer if you win big, so I thought I would—"

East started to grin and then pulled her down on his lap.

"This is good," he said. "In fact, this is great, but will you do me a favor?"

"Of course," she said.

"The next time you feel lucky, take me with you."

She frowned. "Oh, it's not a matter of luck. It's all about—"

East kissed her square on the lips, stopping her explanation. When he stopped, he was breathing hard and wishing to hell he didn't know she was a virgin.

Ally's expression was somewhere between confused and a little bit stunned when East set her back on her feet.

"I need to call Jonah," he said.

"You don't need his permission to make love to me," Ally said.

He grinned. "I don't?"

"Oh, no. Although he told me he wasn't sending me to Condor Mountain to persuade you with sex, he did say to do whatever it took to get you back in action." Then she grinned.

East didn't know whether to be insulted, or glad she was so damned honest. He decided on the latter.

"You just keep that smile on your face and see what it gets you," he mumbled. "Now where's that phone?"

Ally went to retrieve it. As they waited for Jonah to call, they began readying to leave.

"Where do we go from here?" Ally asked.

East pointed to the map. "We'll hit Highway 93 a little northeast of Vegas. We're taking it straight north into Idaho."

Ally sighed. "I hope we're doing the right thing. This feels so out in left field, you know? We know some stuff, but not definite things. For instance, what about that name Jeff left on the floor? This man Bob?

Is he the kidnapper, or just one of the men who took him?''

"I don't know yet, but I can promise you we will, and the first place we're heading is Elmore Todd's hometown of New Township.''

Ally nodded. ''You're right.'' Then she glanced at the bank of equipment in front of her and pulled up a small wheeled stool and sat down.

"What are you going to do?'' East asked.

"Run some stuff. See if I can make connections between what we know and what we're just guessing at.''

Before he could comment Ally's phone began to ring.

It was Jonah.

"Do you have any information?'' he asked, leaving East with no opportunity for a polite greeting of hello.

"Nothing firm, but we're on the road.''

"You need money,'' Jonah said, as of matter of fact.

East grinned and looked at Ally. ''Actually, we don't. Let's just say, I wouldn't advise anyone to play poker with my partner.''

A rare chuckle echoed in East's ear.

"So,'' Jonah said, ''if not money, then what?''

This was where it got tricky. East took a deep breath.

"I need you to really commit treason…at least in the eyes of the world.''

"What the hell?'' Jonah muttered.

"I have reason to believe I will be contacted shortly by someone interested in your downfall. I have no way of knowing if it's who we're looking for, or just someone who works for him. But if the call comes in, I want something incriminating.''

"No,'' Jonah said shortly. ''They can arrest me now on what they've got before I'll do that.''

East had expected this. In fact, he would have been surprised if Jonah had agreed.

"I don't want anything vital sent. Just make it appear that way. Tell the President, or whoever you need to tell to get clearance, but so help me God, if you expect me to do my job, I need that much cooperation from you. I need to trace the communications that are being intercepted, and what better way than to track a piece of top security info."

There was a long stretch of silence. Finally, Jonah answered.

"I will call you back."

The line went dead.

East disconnected, his gut in a knot. If Jonah didn't cooperate, Jeff was as good as dead. And if he told Jonah what was really going on, he would be pulled immediately. Company policy was strict, and Jonah was a company man all the way.

"Is he going to cooperate?" Ally asked, without taking her eyes from the computer screen.

"I hope so," East said, and sat down in the front seat with a thump. "If he doesn't, we're screwed and Jeff's history."

A series of text suddenly popped up on the screen. With a satisfied smile, she began to scroll down the lines, scanning the text as she went.

"Maybe not," she said. "Maybe not."

"What are you into now?" East asked.

"Back in FBI files."

He frowned. "Damn woman, don't they have any safeguards on this stuff?"

"Of course, but I sort of set this file up to begin with, so I know where the back doors are."

"Back doors?"

She glanced up at him and then smiled. "Just trust me."

He gripped her shoulders, giving them a quick squeeze. "Honey, I'm already there."

A couple of minutes passed, in which East paced and she worked. Suddenly, she laughed. He turned to see why.

"Bingo," she said softly.

He leaned over her shoulder, reading the text on the screen. "Militia groups?"

"Look at how many there are," she said.

"What exactly are you looking for here."

"I've cross-referenced the known groups with known members named Bob, and then cross-checked those names to see how many times Elmore Todd's name comes up in conjunction with them."

"Good job," East said. "What did you find?"

Her phone rang before she could answer. She pointed at East.

"You might as well answer that. It will be Jonah for you."

Saying a quick, silent prayer, he answered.

"Yes?"

"Let me know when you want the information," Jonah said.

East went weak with relief. "Thanks."

"It is I who should be thanking you," Jonah said.

A dial tone sounded in East's ear. He disconnected and handed the phone to Ally.

"Buckle up partner. We're heading north."

Jeff moaned in his sleep and woke himself up with the echo of his own voice. His head was hot and achy and it hurt to swallow. When he tried to sit up to get a drink of water, he pitched forward instead, hitting the floor headfirst.

"Son of a bitch," he mumbled, and crawled back to the cot on his hands and knees, then got back in bed.

Every muscle in his body was trembling and something wet was running from his forehead into his hair. He touched the wet spot, then put his finger to his lips and tasted it.

Blood.

A shudder racked his body as he reached for the covers, but felt nothing but air. He had enough medical experience to suspect he was on the verge of pneumonia. The constant chill, the damp, weeping walls and the lack of nourishing food and warmth were all taking their toll.

Almost twenty-four hours after they'd pulled out of the casino parking lot, they stopped at a place just outside of Boaz, Nevada. The sign on the truck stop was peeling and hanging by only one hinge, but the café was still open and they offered hookups for RVs. As tired as East was, it couldn't get much better than that.

Ally hadn't spoken in over three hours and was still in the back, doodling with the notes she'd downloaded. He stood and stretched.

"I'll go see about hookups. Be back in a bit."

She nodded without looking up.

A short while later he came back, moved the RV to the designated location and got out again to hook up the utilities. As he stepped back inside, he saw the concentration on her face, and opted to go buy some dinner. Chances were he'd be back before she ever knew he was gone.

Sometime later, Ally became aware that they'd

stopped moving. She turned to look for East, but he was gone. Shoving aside the files, she stood up, and as she did, stumbled, then sat down in the floor with a thump.

"Oh, great," she mumbled, then started to laugh at herself as she took off her shoes.

East found her on the floor, barefoot and still chuckling. He set aside the food he was carrying and hurried toward her.

"Ally, are you all right?"

"I can't feel my foot. I sat there so long it went to sleep and I didn't even know it."

"Did you fall? Are you hurt?"

"Only my pride. Help me up," then added, "please."

He took her by the hands and pulled, hauling her off her butt and into his arms, then nuzzled the side of her neck before planting a kiss on the side of her cheek.

"Is this foreplay?" she asked.

Her question rocked his intentions. He looked at her and grinned.

"Do you want it to be?"

When she frowned, actually contemplating the question, he grinned.

"If you have to think about it, then your answer should be no," he said. "How about dinner, instead?"

Her eyes widened in appreciation. "Yes, please. I'm starved."

"Wash up," he said. "Hope you like what I chose, and I'll warn you, there's no money in the bottom of my sack, only napkins and ketchup."

She peeked into the sack on her way past, sniffing in appreciation.

"Mmm, hamburgers and fries. Did you put onions on mine?"

"They're loaded," he said. "You can take off whatever you want."

"I don't want to take anything off," she said, and hastened toward the bath.

East watched her go, her hips swaying to a feminine rhythm that only women can hear. He eyed her jeans and her shirt, wondering how long their food would stay hot if he followed his inclinations. She might not want anything removed, but he damn sure did.

Yet when she came back, he was the perfect gentleman, food laid out and waiting for her to dig in. It wasn't until bedtime that things began to sizzle again.

East was lying stretched out on his mattress, his eyes closed and his hands folded beneath his head. The sounds of Ally's shower were all but drowned out by the soft, country tune playing in the background from the clock radio he'd set by his bed. A woman's voice was weaving a plaintive story within the melody about a man who'd done her wrong. His conscience pricked with every note she sang. If he followed his instincts, would he do Ally wrong? He was in love with her. Flat out, deep down in his soul, forever in love. He could think of nothing better than to make a home with her, even make babies with her. But was this dream a selfish one? She was young—not even at the peak of her career with SPEAR. Maybe she didn't want to settle down. He had no idea how she felt about marriage or babies. And if she did come to love him, would she want to retire from active duty? Could he live with the knowledge that at any given time, on any operation, she might never come home.

He rolled over on his belly and gave his pillow a thump, bunching it beneath his chin and closing his eyes. The whole thing was a mess from beginning to end. He couldn't help thinking that if it hadn't been for Jonah, Jeff's life would not be in danger right now. But then, had it not been for Jonah's situation, East would never have met Ally. He thumped his pillow again just to punctuate his frustration. As he did, the song ended and so did Ally's shower. He heard the bathroom door open, then the sound of her bare feet upon the floor. He heard her hesitate, then heard her sigh. A few seconds later, the sound of shifting covers and the mattress scooting a bit on the floor told him that she'd crawled into her own bed. His gut knotted, just thinking about her lying beside him. All he had to do was turn, take her in his arms and—

"Are you asleep?"

He jumped, then stifled a wry grin before raising up on his elbows.

"Not now," he said, looking with great appreciation at the damp tendrils of her hair and her freshly scrubbed face.

Her eyebrows knotted across her forehead. "Well...*were* you asleep before?"

He couldn't find it in himself to lie, even though it would have been easier.

"No, I wasn't asleep."

"Then why pretend?"

He rolled over on his side, raised up on one elbow, and gazed down into those wide, questioning eyes.

"So I don't have to face the fact that I want to make love to you."

Ally sat up, her bare legs crossed, bracing herself with her elbows as she leaned a bit forward.

"But why?"

He sighed. "I want to ask you something. How do you feel about me?"

"I like you very much," she said promptly.

He smiled, but it wasn't what he wanted to hear.

"Thank you, honey, but that's not what I meant." He tried coming at the subject from a different way. "If the only reason you want to make love is because you're curious about the act, then I don't think I'm the man for the job."

"Oh, that's all right," she said quickly. "I think I knew all along that it wouldn't happen. I mean...why would someone like you be interested in an oddball like me...especially in that way?"

She managed a smile, but he saw the pain in her eyes before she looked away. That, above everything else, hurt his heart. He couldn't bear to think that he was causing her pain. So when she lay down with her back to him and pulled the covers up around her shoulders, he kicked his own covers aside, then crawled over to her mattress and stretched out behind her, aligning himself against her backside and then pulling her tightly against him until they were separated by nothing more than a blanket and sheet.

"What do you think you're doing?" Ally muttered.

"I think I'm falling for you," he said softly. "Now go to sleep."

There was a long moment of silence and then Ally started to cry. Not loud, ugly sobs; just quiet tears of joy and disbelief.

East felt her trembling and raised up again and leaned over her, peering intently through the shadows at her face. The glitter of tears on her cheeks made him groan.

"Ally…honey…for God's sake, don't cry. Whatever I said, I take back."

She rolled over on her back and locked her arms around his neck before he could move.

"Don't you dare," she said fiercely. "Nobody has ever said that to me before, so don't you dare take it back."

"Ah sweetheart," East muttered, and slid his hands beneath her shoulders, lifting her close, then closer still. "You have less than ten seconds to change my mind before I show you what this is about."

"Show me," she begged, and lifted her mouth for his kiss.

He did as she asked, starting with the kiss. The covers between them came next as he tossed them aside, then her nightshirt and his gym shorts followed until they were naked to each other's sight. It was her innocence, as much as her charm, that sent his head in a spin.

"Can I touch you?" she whispered.

He grinned wryly. "Honey, you can do anything you damn well please to me and it will be okay."

"Truly?"

He pressed a kiss between her breasts and at the base of her neck, then on the center of her mouth.

"Truly," he said.

She pushed him until he was lying on his back, then splayed her hands across the middle of his chest. When those long, slender fingers began a foray across his chest, then moved lower toward his belly, he took a deep breath. As she hesitated at the juncture of his thighs then encircled him slowly, he gritted his teeth and closed his eyes. Never in his life had he experienced anything as seductive as her hesitant exploration. Within seconds, his manhood began to expand, and as it did, he heard a slight gasp, then a whispered, "Oh my."

He exhaled slowly and looked up. Her gaze was locked upon him, and then on his face. He couldn't tell if she was scared to death, or utterly fascinated by his response to her.

"My turn," he said, and rolled her onto her back before she could argue.

With a tenderness and patience he would not have believed himself capable of, he loved her to the point of insanity. Within minutes, he had her writhing beneath his caress, rocking with the rhythm of his fingers.

Ally's heart was pounding, her blood racing like flood waters toward an overflowing dam. It was at once, the most wonderful and the most frightening thing she had ever experienced. Never in her life had she been so out of control, or so bound to another's spell. The panic that came with it was almost more than she could bear, and it was instinct that made her reach for East, holding on to him to keep from dying.

"Let it go, honey," he whispered. "Just let go. I won't let you fall."

She closed her eyes and gave herself up to the ecstasy, crying aloud in the dark as the sensations shook her from her head to her toes. And when her blood was still hammering between her legs, East slipped in. She never felt the pain of his entry, or her body adjusting to his size. All she knew was that the addictive pounding of that pulse had suddenly restarted itself in a most unbelieving manner.

She opened her eyes to find him above her, looking down at her with love on his face. She lifted her arms to him, pulling him down until his weight was pressing her through the mattress to the floor, and it was still not close enough. Bits and pieces of things that she'd read began to filter through her mind as she yearned to give back to him that most wonderful thing that he'd just given her. She shifted slightly and lifted her legs, wrapping them around his waist and pulling him even closer still.

He groaned. And when she moved again, then again, then again, he groaned even more. To her joy, she could feel him coming undone and the power of his release filled her long-empty heart.

When East could talk without stuttering, he rolled, taking her with him and holding her close.

"Wow," he said. "I thought you'd never done this before."

She smiled against the warmth of his chest and snuggled a little bit closer.

"I read a book," she stated.

"Have mercy. You read all that in a book?"

She nodded.

He managed a grin, thinking to himself that he'd just possibly uncovered the mother lode.

"And what book would that have been?"

"It was actually two. One was the *Kama Sutra,* and the other was by a retired madame from the Chicken Ranch in Nevada."

East started to laugh.

Embarrassed, Ally tried to pull away, but East

stopped her, holding her even closer and then smothering her face with kisses.

"What is so funny?" she finally managed to ask.

"You are the most marvelous mix of femininity I've ever encountered in my life, and all I can say is...education is a wonderful thing."

Chapter 13

"The time is seven o'clock and if you're heading out to work early, there is a wreck at the off-ramp of Interstate 80 and Highway 93. The eastbound lanes of I-80 are partially blocked, so take it slow out there people, and keep it safe."

Ally rolled over on her back, groaning in disbelief at the cheery voice of the radio host as the clock radio East had set last night came on. When she saw him reach for the Off button without opening his eyes, she grinned and impulsively crawled around the mattress, scooting it a little farther out of his reach as the host continued his spiel with an update on the day's weather.

"On the home front today, the temperatures are predicted to reach the high seventies, with a nighttime low of forty-four."

East muttered beneath his breath and slapped toward the sound. The radio kept playing.

Ally stifled a fit of giggles as she watched him open his eyes reluctantly, in search of the offending noise.

"In national news, the Grand Jury testimony contin- ues on Capitol Hill and members of the ATF are ex- pected to testify before the day is out. It is rumored that certain agents of the U.S. Treasury will be called. It's difficult to say what the IRS could possibly have to add to the testimony of the ATF agents, so it looks as if it will be a case of wait and see."

Ally had been too focused on her fun with East to pay much attention to what was being broadcast until something the announcer said suddenly clicked. She sat up with a start and then bounced to her feet, dashing over East's body to the console where the hard copies of the information she'd downloaded were lying.

East opened his eyes just in time to see Ally vault over his legs. He sat up with a jerk, looking around for his gun while the radio continued to play.

"In Hollywood, insiders are saying—"

East reached for the radio, slapping the Off button and tossing it against the wall as he bolted up from where they'd been sleeping.

"What's going on? Is something wrong?"

She was slinging papers and files, moving mouse pads and pens, digging through the accumulation of information that they'd been gathering for days, all the while muttering.

"Bob...it's not really Bob after all. Where did I put those...I thought they were...never mind, here they are."

"Who's not Bob?"

Then the moment he asked it, he knew what she meant. The name Jeff had left on the floor of his apart- ment. If it wasn't Bob, then who?

Ally headed back to the mattress where she knelt and began sorting the pages out around her. East knelt beside her, watching and trying, without success, to figure out what she was doing.

Suddenly, she slapped her knee with the flat of her hand.

"I knew it!" she crowed, snatching a paper from one stack and adding it to the one she was holding.

"Let me in on the news."

"What if Bob isn't Bob, but an acronym?"

"For what?"

She handed him the papers in her hand.

"Read for yourself. Elmore Todd was in Jeff's house. We know that from the fingerprint. And Elmore Todd is a known militia sympathizer. We know that from his priors. And…Elmore Todd is a native of Idaho, which is where we believe Jeff is being held."

"Yes, but what does—"

"I'm getting to that," Ally said, all but clapping her hands with glee. "Bob. All this time, we thought Bob was one of the kidnapper's names, but what if it's not?"

She got to her knees and pointed to separate lines on each of the pages in East's hands.

"Elmore Todd has been tied to three different militia groups in the last twenty-one years—America's Freemen, Sons of Glory, and the Brotherhood of Blood. *B. O. B.* Bob."

East rocked back on his heels. It had been there all the time. He looked at Ally, then shook his head in disbelief.

"How did you figure this out?" Then he shook his head. "Never mind. I don't need to know. It's enough that you did."

"So you think I'm right?" she asked.

East grinned. "Honey, after last night, I'm never going to question your ability to do anything again."

She smiled prettily, blushing the least little bit as she began gathering the papers she'd scattered.

"What can we do with this information?" she asked.

"We can skip going to New Township to look for Elmore Todd. Instead, we need to find out where the Brotherhood of Blood is keeping house and find a way to pay them a visit."

She frowned. "I don't like that. We're severely outnumbered."

"So's Jeff," East growled, then grabbed her from behind and rolled, taking her with him. "And right now, so are you."

They fell in the middle of the mattresses with paper scattered all around them and began to renew the discoveries they'd made last night.

"Know any more of those tricks?" East asked.

"Oh, yes, I believe there are thirty-five chapters in the *Kama Sutra* and last night was worth only a couple of pages."

He grinned. "I have a few tricks of my own," he said. "Wanna trade?"

Three days later, they were no closer to finding Jeff. All of their leads had run into nothing and not even flashing their badges at the Idaho Bureau of Investigation had given them access to the Brotherhood of Blood. It was, according to the bureau chief, one of the few survivalist groups in the state that stayed on the move. They'd been flushed out of national park areas only to reappear months later in another area of the state. The last two reports the bureau had were over nine months old. For a group bent on revolt, they maintained a remarkably low profile, which according to the chief, made them more dangerous than most. His comment to East had been telling, and East couldn't get it out of his mind.

He'd said, "Big dogs bark and snarl and make a lot of noise, but it's those little dogs that come around behind you when you're not expecting it that will bite you in the ass."

So the Brotherhood didn't spread themselves as thinly as others. So they kept to themselves and if they were responsible for myriad dirty deeds, they kept the glory to themselves. So if this was so, how in hell was East supposed to find them?

After what seemed to be an endless drive, they parked *Baby* at a KOA campground outside of Ketchum that night and settled down to wait for the kidnapper's call. East's plan was to demand to speak to Jeff again and then try and trace the call, hoping to pinpoint the Brotherhood's location. The state was too vast and too desolate to just strike out on a mile-by-mile search. Far too many areas of the state were accessible only by boat or by air. Waiting was risky, but it was their only option. Waiting with Ally had become a risky business of its own. Day by day, they worked head-to-head—by night, they slept in each other's arms. For East, life was getting more complicated by the minute.

Ally was blossoming in a way she would have never believed. When she looked at herself in a mirror, she saw a woman in love. Each day that she awoke beside East was a day closer to heaven. She didn't think past the time when this case would be over. She couldn't let herself face what her future might be. East had said nothing about what he was feeling, save the fact that he loved to make love to her. That much she already knew from the wild, crazy nights they spent in each other's arms. What she wanted—no, needed—was to know that he truly loved her—that when this was over, their relationship would still exist.

Yet, as badly as she needed to hear this, pressing him now when his son's life was at stake seemed insensitive. So she laughed with him, argued with him, and at night, made love with him and let it be enough.

The next day, at four minutes after six in the evening, East's phone began to ring. It was what they'd been waiting for, and yet they both stared without moving at the small, black appliance as if it had grown fangs. Suddenly, Ally bolted toward the equipment and hit the controls. East grabbed the phone, then looked to see if Ally was on the trace. When she nodded, he answered.

"This is Kirby."

"I was beginning to think you'd lost interest, my friend."

The urge to kill was so strong East could feel it in his bones. Instead of reacting to his rage, he took a deep breath, then answered in a sarcastic drawl.

"I'm not your friend and where is my son?"

A low chuckle from the kidnapper rattled his poise.

"There's something you haven't realized. You're not calling the shots. Now what do you have for me? Something special, I hope. I don't want you to disappoint me again."

East glanced at Ally. She was motioning for him to continue.

"I have what you asked for, but I want to talk to my son first. Then I'll give you the details."

There was a sharp intake of breath on the other end of the line, then an angry snarl.

"That won't do. I'm tired of playing games with you. I want my information now or your son dies."

East clenched a fist, but he kept on talking.

"I don't give you a damn thing until I know my son is still alive. You don't have to like it, buddy, but that's the way I play."

The line went dead in his ear.

"Did you get anything?" he asked.

Ally shook her head. "Nothing that will help, although I can tell you for certain that was an international call."

"You mean he's not even in the U.S.?"

"Not today," she said.

"Call Jonah, and hurry. I need the information now before the kidnapper calls back."

Seconds later, she made the call, then hung up. All they could do was wait. Within two minutes, Jonah was on the phone.

"It's going down," East said. "Give me something…fast."

Jonah rattled off a series of names and codes that made East's hair stand on end. Even though he knew this was false information, just the thought of giving away the identities of double agents abroad made him sick to his stomach.

"You're sure it's okay to use these?" he asked.

"Last week it would have meant their death. Today they've already been relocated and their codes have been changed."

"Okay," East said. "We'll see what we see."

Jonah hesitated, then added, ''He's got to be stopped.''

''I'm doing the best I can,'' East said.

Jonah disconnected.

A moment of guilt came and went, then East shook it off. Nothing mattered but Jeff. He turned to Ally, who was still on the trace.

''Out of curiosity, did you get a lock on that call?'' he asked.

She grinned. ''The moon.''

''Hell of a scrambler he's got on that thing.''

She laughed.

East's phone rang again. He pointed to Ally, counted down with his fingers; three…two…one. They picked up at the same time and the trace began.

Caleb Carpenter came out of the Brotherhood head-quarters on the run with a cell phone in his hand.

''Get the hostage out of the hole! Now!'' he yelled, motioning toward three nearby men.

Immediately, they dropped the guns they'd been cleaning and ran toward the hole. Within moments, the door was lifted and for the first time in many, many days, light spilled across the flat, concrete floor. One of the men leaned down and shouted.

''Hey boy! Get yourself up here on the double!''

Nothing moved and no one answered.

By now, Caleb was at the hole and peering down.

''Hey, smart-mouth. Your old man wants to reach out and touch. Don't you want to talk to him?''

Caleb could just see the foot of the cot and thought he saw something move.

''Wake the hell up!'' he shouted.

This time, they heard a distinct groan. At the sound,

Caleb's heart skipped a beat. God almighty, the success of everything they were doing involved keeping him alive.

"Get down there now," he ordered. "But watch yourselves. He could be faking."

They thumped down the steps in rapid succession. But the first man had barely hit the bottom step when he stopped and turned, his expression panicky as he yelled back at Caleb.

"Sir! This doesn't look good!"

Caleb cursed beneath his breath and took the steps down, two at a time.

Jeff Kirby was almost unrecognizable. The heavy growth of whiskers on his face, along with a blood-caked forehead and lack of color beneath his skin, was proof enough to Caleb that they were all in big trouble. He felt Jeff's skin. The kid was burning with fever. A dark frown cut between Caleb's eyebrows, mirroring the lines that deepened beside his mouth. He turned.

"Where's Anderson? He was supposed to be taking care of the hostage."

They looked at each other then shrugged. "Not sure, sir. Maybe in the mess hall."

"Find him," he snapped. "Do it now."

One of the men bolted up the steps, while Caleb motioned for the others to come closer.

"Get him up and on his feet," he said. "He's got to make this call."

When a flood of light suddenly pierced the dark, Jeff thought he was dreaming. But when it persisted, and he could see vague shadows coming toward him and silhouetted against the light, he decided that he'd finally died and was on his way to heaven. It wasn't until he heard someone curse that he figured he'd made a mistake.

"Water," he mumbled.

Someone lifted a cup to his dry, cracked lips, and although the water went in his mouth, his throat was too swollen to swallow.

"Son of a bitch," someone muttered, as they dragged him to his feet.

Jeff shook his head. "Not in heaven," he mumbled.

"Not by a long shot, boy," Caleb said. "But I'll send you to hell myself if you don't do as I say."

"Already there," he muttered, as his legs gave way.

"Get him up the steps and into the sun," Caleb ordered.

The two men all but dragged Jeff up the steps. Then when he would have fallen again, Caleb ordered them to sit him on the top step instead. Gratefully, Jeff sat with his head in his hands and his eyes tightly closed, unable to bear the motion of movement, or the bright, sunlit sky.

"You're going to talk to Daddy, do you hear me?" Caleb asked. "You're going to tell him everything's fine or so help me, I'll break your stubborn neck myself."

"Go to hell," Jeff muttered and took a shaky swing at the blur before him.

Caleb dodged the feeble blow then punched in a series of numbers, waiting for the call to be answered.

East picked up on the first ring. "This is Kirby."

Caleb glanced down at Jeff, wondering how this was going to play out. All he could do was hope for the best.

"You have thirty seconds. Say what you want to

your son and get it over with. The boss isn't happy with you.''

''Well, hell,'' East drawled. ''I'm not too happy with him, either. Now let me talk to Jeff.''

Caleb put the phone to Jeff's ear. ''Talk,'' he ordered.

Jeff felt the pressure of plastic against his face and moved his mouth toward the sensation.

''Dad?''

The word was barely audible, and East's heart almost stopped.

''Jeff? Jeff? Are you all right?''

East sounded so far away. Jeff reached for the phone, wanting to put it closer to his ear.

Reluctantly, Caleb released it, and he would look back on that action later with regret.

''Dad...''

Then the world started to spin. Jeff felt himself fading but couldn't find the words to speak. He pitched forward, rolling headfirst down the steps like a broken toy, and taking the phone with him. It hit the concrete a second before Jeff did, and then slid out of sight. Jeff's groan was loud and long, and then unconsciousness took him.

Caleb saw him falling and grabbed at Jeff's shirt. But it slipped through his fingers, leaving him to watch in dismay as the phone and the kid went flying.

''Grab him, damn it!''

But his order came too late. Both Jeff and the phone were gone.

East could only listen in horror, trying to imagine what was happening. Never in his life had he felt as helpless. He turned to Ally, giving her a frantic look, but she was focused on the computer terminal. The only good thing to come from it all was the phone. The line was still open. The trace was almost done.

He gripped the phone until his knuckles were white, listening intently, trying to pinpoint a recognizable sound that might help them locate Jeff, but all he could hear was a string of virulent curses, and someone named Anderson catching a large dose of hell.

A minute passed, and then suddenly Ally jumped to her feet and grabbed East, silently pointing to the screen and giving him a thumbs up.

East's shoulders slumped. Even though they'd traced the call, it didn't mean Jeff would be alive when they got there.

Suddenly, there was a breathless voice in his ear.

"Are you there? Are you there?"

"I'm here, you sorry bastard. What the hell have you done to my son?"

"We did nothing," Caleb said. "He fell. He's fine. Just confused."

"No, you're confused," East shouted. "You get nothing. Your sorry-ass boss gets nothing. Nothing goes from me to you without proof that Jeff is still alive." Then he hung up in Caleb Carpenter's ear.

"Damn," Caleb muttered. Then he pointed to Jeff. "Get him out of the hole and into the infirmary. Have Henry take a look at him. See what he can do," then he stomped up the steps, aware that they were bound to get another call from the boss and he wouldn't be happy.

But Caleb wasn't the only one who was nervous about a call. East knew he was playing fast and loose by making demands, and he had heard Jeff's voice just before everything hit the fan. What he did know was that, sick or hurt, Jeff was in trouble and they had to get him out fast.

Within minutes, the call came that East had been waiting for. The kidnapper's fury was evident as he screamed into the phone.

"You messed up and signed your kid's death warrant."

East was shaking with an equal rage and a fast growing fear that the man was right.

"He couldn't even talk to me," East shouted back. "You don't keep your word, I have no reason to keep mine."

The kidnapper let loose with a long string of curses, promising every dire consequence to every member of East's family for the next fifty years.

East's laugh was short and bitter. "Jeff was my only family member, you stupid son of a bitch. There's no one left you can hurt."

"There's you," the kidnapper snarled.

"Come and get me," East said, and hung up.

The phone rang again within seconds.

"What?" East snapped.

It was as if East was talking to an entirely different man. The fury—the rage—the incoherence was completely gone from the kidnapper's voice.

"This is all a misunderstanding," he said. "Your son is ill, but he's being doctored as we speak. He has not been harmed, now give me what I want."

"And if I do, when will you give me my son?"

"Well now," the man chuckled. "That's a little different. I've decided that he's a pretty good nest egg for me. I'll give you your son back, when I take Jonah down. I'll call you within a week or so for new information, and I promise you another call to your son will be forthcoming. What do you say?''

Aware that he'd played out this hand, East blurted out the information that Jonah had given him. Seconds later, a dial tone buzzed in his ear.

He disconnected, then tossed the phone aside and strode out of the RV without saying a word.

Ally followed, catching up with him at the edge of a cluster of trees. East was pale and shaking, but when she looked at his face, she saw it was rage and not fear that was holding him hostage.

She grabbed him by the forearms, making him face her—making him listen.

''Whatever he said, it doesn't matter. Turn loose of that anger and help me. I've got the location of the call. I've even got the number of the cell phone from where it was made. We can find Jeff. We can do it.''

He closed his eyes and took a deep breath. When he opened them, she was still there—waiting. A calm came over him then and he knew before this went any further, she had to know what her presence meant to him.

''Come here,'' he said, and held out his hand, pulling her to a nearby bench where they sat.

Ally waited, unable to imagine what he must be feeling. When he palmed her hand between the breadth of his own, she looked up at him and smiled.

He leaned forward until their foreheads were touching. He kissed her cheek, then her lips. As always, the tentative blend of woman and innocence left him weak.

''The day Jeff was kidnapped was the worst and the best day of my life. I was afraid and confused, uncertain of where to start, and then I turned around and you were there. 'We'll find him,' you said, and at that moment, I knew it was true. Ever since the day you came into my life, I've been fighting an emotion I will no longer deny. I am in love with you, sweetheart...deeply and without reservation, and I am going to love you forever, whether it matters to you or not.''

"Oh, East," Ally whispered, then stood up and stepped between his legs, wrapping her arms around his neck and pulling his head to her breasts. "I love you, too.''

He held her there, with his cheek against the beat of her heart and knew a peace like he'd never known before.

For Ally, the last of her misgivings about herself disappeared. Safe in the assurance of East Kirby's love, she had become a confident and loving woman. Together, they could do anything—and they needed to find his son to make their family complete.

"How do you want to approach this?" Ally said.

"Geographically speaking, exactly where did the call originate?"

"The Bitterroots," she said, and then sat down on his knee as they began to make plans.

East frowned. Those mountains were desolate and unpopulated. There was no way they could come in without warning. "How close did we get?"

"I'm guessing it's about a mile radius in which we'll have to search," Ally replied.

"We'll fly the area. There's bound to be buildings of some sort that are visible from the air."

"We'll need a pilot and a—"

"I'm certified to fly just about anything shy of a jumbo jet," East said.

"I am impressed."

He gave her a lopsided smile. "And you should be,"

he teased. "I am an impressive kind of guy." Then he lifted her off his lap and stood. "Let's get cracking. I can't get rid of the feeling that Jeff's life hinges on how quickly we can find him."

Chapter 14

The next day they were in the air at daybreak, heading north. They'd been flying a little over two hours, and for Ally, the two-seater plane they were in was like skimming the heavens in a toy. Ally was scanning the aerial map in her lap, searching for landmarks when she suddenly tapped East's arm and then motioned for him to look down.

"Anywhere within this area. Look for rooftops. A road. Anything that indicates inhabitation."

He nodded and began to bank, taking the plane into a circle. At first they saw nothing below but the mountains, scrub brush and a vast endless canyon with a thin ribbon of reddish-brown water threaded through it. It wasn't until he began a second sweep through the area that a flash of sunlight on something below caught his eye. Unwilling to fly lower, he motioned for Ally to use her binoculars. She could see a series of rooftops, a couple of vehicles, and what appeared to be a single-track road leading into the area. After one quick look, she checked the coordinates on the map in her lap, then looked again.

"That's got to be it," she said. "There's nothing else out here, and these are the coordinates from which the call was made."

He glanced at the fuel gauge, then at his watch. "There's no place to land a plane like this. We'll need a chopper."

"And I have an idea that might make our retrieval easier," Ally added.

He nodded, looking down at the area one last time. *Hang in there, son. I'll be back.* Then he nosed the plane south.

East sat cross-legged on the floor of the RV, listening to the tape Ally was playing for him. Even though he'd watched her doing it, he was stunned at the authenticity of the piece.

"So, what do you think?" she asked.

"I think it's genius. Play it again, will you?"

She hit Rewind, then Play, listening along with East to the kidnapper's voice.

"I'm tired of playing games with you. You messed up. I'm sending my people to retrieve my package. Have it ready and don't disappoint me again."

"Of course, this all hinges on our theory that the people holding Jeff did not expect him to fade out on them or they would never have given him the phone," East said. "It also follows that the kidnapper had to be ticked at them, too, because it messed up his plans with me."

"I agree," Ally said. "You're sure it was Jeff's voice that you heard?"

East nodded, eyeing her with renewed respect. "You're damn good at what you do, aren't you, Ally?"

"Without tooting my own horn too loudly, I'll say yes."

"Before, I would have said our chances of rescuing Jeff without a small army were slim to none, but this could be the key to getting in and out of there without force."

She grinned. "That and a woman with attitude."

"What do you mean?"

"Well, it stands to reason that a woman who would work for this kidnapper is not going to be on any debutante list. And since you're the pilot, I will be the one ostensibly sent on retrieval detail."

A quick frown furrowed across East's forehead. "Now wait a minute, you don't think I'm going to sit in the background while you—"

"I don't think it, I know it," she said. "You're too emotionally involved in this to stay cool. Besides, the less show of force, the less the men holding Jeff will suspect."

East shook his head. "I don't like it. There are too many unknowns."

"That's what the assault rifles are for…changing people's minds. Now let's call Jonah."

A few minutes later, after going through the same procedure as always, Ally's cell phone rang. She answered.

"This is Corbin."

"Good evening, Alicia, I trust all is well?"

"Yes, sir, going quite nicely, sir. We need some supplies."

"Name them."

"An unmarked chopper, preferably a Bell Jet

Ranger, two assault rifles and ammunition, camouflage gear for two, size ten women's and a man's extra large. Shoe sizes eight for me, twelve for East. Oh…and just for effect, why don't you throw in a gun and holster for me, something big, ugly and deadly.''

"That's quite a list, young lady. Are you sure you've been all that good this year.''

Ally's eyes widened in surprise. To hear Jonah joking about being Santa Claus, even briefly, was not in the context with which she normally dealt.

"Yes, sir, I believe that I have,'' she said.

He chuckled softly, then his demeanor changed. "What's going down?''

"We have reason to believe we've located some associates, although we have no way of knowing if the target will be present.''

"This is good. Do you require any backup?''

Ally glanced at East. "Not at the present, although as you know, I'm not the primary on this, sir.''

"Right. Let me talk to East.''

"Yes, sir. I'll put him on.'' She handed the phone to East.

"This is Kirby.''

"What's going down?''

"We've located what we believe to be known associates, and while we have no identity on your target, there is the possibility that he could be among them.''

"Do what you need to do,'' Jonah said.

East thought of Jeff. "Yes, sir. Never doubt that is exactly what I'm doing.''

"Where and when do you want the deliveries?'' Jonah asked.

East gave him the time and coordinates.

"It's done,'' Jonah said. "And good luck.''

"Thank you, sir. We're going to need it."

He disconnected, then handed the phone to Ally for safekeeping.

"Hopefully, the next time we talk to Jonah, it will be with good news," Ally said.

East shook his head. "I doubt it. Not when he learns I've been deceiving him."

Ally frowned. "It's not deception in the true sense of the word. These people *are* associated with the man who's trying to ruin Jonah. Locating them will give Jonah new information. Who knows where it will go from there?"

East shrugged. "It won't be how he perceives it, but I can't let anything matter but getting my son out alive." He got to his feet and began to pace. "Waiting for daylight is going to be hell."

Ally put her hand on his shoulder, then cupped the side of his face.

"I have an idea," she said softly.

"What?"

"After dinner, I know a good way to burn off some energy."

East sighed and then smiled, thinking of that wonderful book that she'd read.

"Yeah, I could go for that," he said, and gave her a quick hug. "What sounds good to eat?"

"Oh, I don't care," she said. "It's what comes afterward that really matters."

East grunted as Ally body-slammed him onto his butt and drove to the basket with a look of glee on her face. All he could do was watch in dismay at the perfection of her layup. The basketball went through the net in a near-silent swish and she thrust her hands sky-ward as she laughed and turned.

"That's game!" she crowed. "I win."

"You cheated," he muttered, as she helped him to his feet.

"I did no such thing," she said. "I even offered to spot you four points but you refused."

"I didn't want to take unfair advantage of you, since I'm almost a foot taller. How was I to know you were a hustler?"

"I do not hustle," she said haughtily, and retrieved her ball before striding to a nearby bench to get her towel and bottle of water.

"Like hell," East said, as he followed her there, watching as she downed her drink.

Behind them, the dusk-to-dawn streetlights at the municipal park were just coming on and a quartet of young men was approaching the court.

"Thank God," he muttered. "Reinforcements."

She turned, eyeing the boys with curiosity. "I thought you were ready to call it quits."

"I never quit," he said shortly. "However, it would be rude to hog the only court."

She laughed. "Admit it. Their arrival saved your butt from having to play me again."

He grinned, ruefully rubbing his posterior. "No, they arrived too late to save the butt to which you so politely refer, but they did give me a good excuse to take you home."

Impulsively, Ally threw her arms around his neck and kissed him soundly. Just when he was getting into the act, she withdrew.

"Not that I'm complaining," East said. "But what was that for?"

"For being a good sport, and for offering to show me your etchings."

He leaned forward, whispering so they wouldn't be overheard. "I didn't say a damn thing about showing you etchings."

She grinned. "That's right, you didn't. However, surely you can find something of interest to show me before the night is through."

East laughed out loud. "Woman, it's just possible that you could be the death of me...but if that's so, then what a way to go."

Night had come to Ketchum, Idaho, blanketing *Baby* and her inhabitants in varying degrees of shadows. An assortment of flying insects hammered themselves at the blue-white night-lights of the RV park while traffic sped by on the highway beyond. Inside the psychedelic RV, another kind of frenzy had evolved. One born of love and desperation, and an acceptance that tomorrow, should something go wrong, this could be their last night on earth. And while none of these fears had been voiced, East and Ally knew well the realities of what they were about to do. On this night, making love was their affirmation to each other and to the blessing of still being alive. But long after the passion had subsided and they lay replete and quiet in each other's arms, it was impossible for either of them to ignore the possibility that Jeff Kirby might already be beyond earthly joys.

"Around this next curve and we'll be there," East said, referring to the location he'd given Jonah last night.

Ally nodded, her mind on everything that had yet to

be done. The doctored tape of the kidnapper's demand was in her pocket and a cosmetic bag with a few tricks of the trade lay on the floor beside her feet. Getting into the persona of another person was something she'd done many times now, but never had it seemed as important as it did on this day.

"Hot damn, Jonah came through with a bang," East muttered.

Ally looked up. There was a nondescript man in the clearing ahead, standing beside a gleaming black chopper. Off to his right was an older model truck with a load of feed in the bed. She suspected his innocent appearance was deceptive.

"Did you suspect that he wouldn't?" she asked.

"No, but you forget, it's been ten years since I've played this game. Some things fade with time."

She eyed him carefully, judging his state of mind. He seemed cool, almost indifferent—proper behavior for a man about to go into battle.

"And some things don't."

He nodded, unaware that she was referring to him.

After a brief identification, the man left, claiming he needed to feed his cattle, leaving East and Ally alone. She sorted through the duffle bags inside the chopper, tossing East his clothing, then began unbuttoning her own clothes. Soon, her jeans, tennis shoes and shirt had been replaced with camouflage clothing and black combat boots. Oblivious to everything now but her game plan, she reached for the makeup bag.

East was dressed and buckling his belt when he turned to check Ally's progress. He stopped short, stunned by the transformation. Her eyes had been outlined in something dark and thick, her lips a slash of red in a cold, pale face. She'd slicked some kind of gel through her hair, then combed it away from her face in a mannish style and was in the act of fastening a holster. It hung down the side of her right hip, putting the butt of the gun close at hand.

"Ally?"

She turned. "What?"

His face was expressionless. "Just wanted to see if it was you."

She smiled, and in that moment, he saw the woman he loved, and a feeling of peace settled in.

"Are you ready to make the call?"

She nodded. "Let me get the stuff."

Shuffling through her gear, she produced East's cell phone and the tape. Once more, she punched Play, just to make sure that the tape was in the correct position, then gave East a nod.

"Let 'er rip," he muttered.

Mentally thanking the technology that had allowed her to track and trace those incoming calls, she punched in the number she'd picked up from the Bitterroot area and waited for someone to answer.

Caleb Carpenter was in the middle of his second cup of coffee when his cell phone rang. He frowned and glanced at his watch. He wasn't expecting any calls, although the fit the boss had thrown yesterday after the fiasco with the hostage had given him a rather sleepless night. He cleared his throat and then answered.

"Hello?"

There was a moment of silence, then a voice came over the line that sent a cold chill up his spine.

"I'm tired of playing games with you. You messed up. I'm sending my people to retrieve my package. Have it ready and don't disappoint me again."

"But—"

The line went dead.

He cursed softly and tossed the phone on the desk. This wasn't good. This wasn't good at all. He stood abruptly and headed for the door to check on the hostage. Although they'd filled him full of antibiotics last night before they'd put him back in the hole, he couldn't help but worry. God help them all if the damn kid died.

East and Ally were in the air before eight o'clock that morning and heading north to the Bitterroots with a prayer in their hearts. Pulling this off depended upon the success of a very fragile chain of events.

The supposition that the place they'd seen yesterday was truly the stronghold of the Brotherhood of Blood and the place where Jeff was being held.

The fact that the Brotherhood had no way of communicating with the kidnapper unless he happened to call on them, therefore eliminating the possibility of anyone at the Brotherhood calling to confirm the call they had made.

The hope that Jeff would still be alive to rescue.

A faith that the Brotherhood would accept Ally's authority over their own.

It wasn't something a wise man would bet on, but it was all they had.

East pushed the chopper to its limit while steadying his anxiety with the knowledge that, one way or another, this nightmare would soon be over.

Ally sat quietly, marking time as she settled into her persona as the kidnapper's mouthpiece.

All too soon, the familiar landmarks of their appointed location began to appear. When the rooftops of the compound came into view, East circled it once, making sure that the people below were not taken by surprise.

"Here they come," he said, watching as tiny figures came spilling out of buildings like beans out of a can.

"Take it in," Ally said. "I'm ready to play dirty."

He shifted the controls and the chopper began its descent, dropping straight into the enemy's lap.

The moment Caleb heard the chopper, he knew they were here. He grabbed his gun and came out on the run, waving the other men back who had begun to assemble. The air about them swirled like a wayward twister, blasting them with debris as the chopper dropped into their midst. Caleb jammed his cap a little tighter and turned his head, shielding his eyes. When he finally turned to look, he saw a woman getting out. His eyes widened. This wasn't what he'd expected.

East grabbed Ally's arm as she reached for the door. Their gazes locked.

"I'm here if you need me."

"Oh, I need you all right. I can't fly this damned thing, so don't go and do anything crazy and get yourself hurt or killed, or we're all skunked. Understand?"

He nodded.

"There's something else," Ally added.

"What?"

"Thank you for showing me how special it is to be a woman."

East paled. This sounded too much like a goodbye.

"You just keep your damned self in one piece, because I haven't even started," he warned.

"Love you, too," she said softly, then she turned,

letting herself slide into that cold, hard place inside her mind. She shifted the strap on her assault rifle to a more comfortable place on her shoulder, slid a pair of sunglasses up her nose, then opened the door and jumped out.

She moved through the blowing debris with a purposeful stride, making no attempt to duck beneath the spinning rotors as people are tempted to do, nor did she turn from the dust that must have been blowing in her eyes. Her rifle was aimed at the ground in deference to propriety, but her hand was resting lightly on the place above the trigger. It was impossible to mistake her intent. When she was within a dozen yards of the silent crowd, a man separated himself and stepped forward.

Ah, the man in charge.

She strode forward with a swagger, shoving her femininity into their faces and daring them to test her.

"I came for the package," she said. "Where's it at?"

Caleb frowned. "You're not who we expected."

She slid her hand a little closer along the gun butt, making sure they saw her intent.

"Yeah, and you're not what we expected, either," she snapped. "The boss isn't happy and I didn't come here to debate this with you. I'm following orders, and if you're smart, you will, too."

"Simon still owes us the last half of the money," Caleb snapped.

Ally's heart skipped a beat. Damn. Something they hadn't counted on. But they hadn't come this far to wimp out now.

"You've got nerve," she drawled. "Screwing up a vital piece of business and expecting to still get paid."

She took a step closer, putting herself in his face. "If I were you," she said softly. "I would kiss my own ass and consider myself fortunate I still had the breath to do it."

Caleb hesitated, then turned around. "Anderson...Franklin...go get the kid."

Two men ran off to do his bidding while Ally stood in their midst. The only thing that kept her from panic was the gun on her shoulder and the man at her back. She wouldn't let herself think of what East must be feeling. Staying in this mind-set was imperative to the success of their mission.

She could not see where the two men went, but East could, and when they began dragging back a drop cloth, revealing a door in the ground, his mind went blank. All he could think was that all this time Jeff had already been buried...but buried alive.

The men disappeared in the hole then came up quickly, all but dragging a figure between them. Even though East knew it was Jeff, he would never have recognized him. His blond hair was dark and matted, he suspected with dried blood. His face was heavy with a growth of whiskers, and his features were bruised and swollen. He staggered when he walked, evidence of his weak state, and it was all East could do not to bail out of the chopper and go get him.

When the crowd parted, a muscle in Ally's eye began to twitch. It was her only concession to the shock she felt.

"Load him up," she said, motioning with the barrel of her rifle toward the waiting chopper.

Caleb hesitated, then nodded to the men, who began walking then dragging Jeff along between them.

Ally gave Caleb a last look, making sure he knew

who was in charge, then, resisting the urge to run,
strolled back through the thick, swirling dust as if she
were going to the beach.

Blinded by the sun and swirling dust, it was all Jeff
could do to keep moving. The urge to see what was
happening was overwhelming, but impossible. The
knowledge that he was being moved from the only
place he'd told his father to look made him panic, but
there was nothing he could do to stop the inevitable.

"What's happening?" he mumbled.

"Shut up, and keep moving," someone yelled in his
ear.

He did as they said. Then he heard a woman's voice
behind him just as they thrust him forward.

"Put another bruise on him and you'll wear one just
like it," she yelled.

He didn't know who she was, but if he'd had enough
spit to talk, he would have thanked her.

Suddenly, the swirl of dust was outside and he was
in, lying flat on some kind of floor. He rolled over on
his back and covered his eyes with his hands, shielding
them from the unyielding glare of the sun.

"Scoot your butt," the woman said, and gave him
a shove.

Seconds later a door slammed, shutting out dust and
part of the noise. Jeff rolled again and started to shiver.
His fever was up.

East wanted nothing more than to get out of his seat
and take Jeff in his arms, but they weren't out of the
woods yet. The crowd of men was shifting.

"Is he in?" East yelled.

Ally gave him a thumbs-up. "Yes, East, your boy is
in. Now take us home."

Jeff flinched as the chopper began its ascent. He groaned beneath his breath, convinced he was hallucinating, because he could have sworn he just heard East's voice. The he felt the woman's breath on his face.

"Jeff, honey...you're going to be all right."

Honey? He opened his eyes, shading them with his hands, and looked up into an unfamiliar face.

"Who?" he whispered.

Ally tapped East on the shoulder. "He wants to know who we are."

East glanced out the side of the window to the disappearing landscape far below, then over his shoulder to the young man on the floor. For the first time in a month, he felt like crying for joy, but all he could do was grin.

"Just tell him he's going home."

Chapter 15

Guilt weighed heavily on East's conscience as he watched Jeff sleep. He wasn't the same man they'd rescued yesterday. His color was improving, as was his breathing. His body had been washed, as had his hair, and the beard was gone. Asleep, he looked like a kid again, but East knew that in surviving, Jeff had crossed a threshold into manhood that few would ever know.

He turned suddenly as the door behind him opened, but relaxed just as quickly when he saw that it was Ally.

"How's he doing?" she asked, and gave East a quick kiss on the cheek.

"Good. Still sleeping a lot, though."

"That's the medicine. He needs it. Pneumonia isn't something to scoff at, especially under those conditions."

"I know. We were lucky," he said.

"We were blessed," Ally amended, then blurted out

her news before she lost her nerve. "I have another assignment."

"No," East groaned, and then caught himself. Just because he saw their lives going one way, didn't mean she agreed. He would never ask a woman to give up a career for him. "Sorry," he said gruffly. "That just slipped out."

Ally wanted to cry. "Don't apologize," she said. "It's what I said when Jonah called."

East sighed. "What did he say about all of this?"

"Not what you would expect. He seemed horrified about what had happened to your family because of him and said to tell you that he would never impose upon you like that again. Then he wished you good luck at the resort and something about a long and happy life."

East looked away. "I lied to him. It's not something I'm proud of."

"I don't think he considered it a lie, East. You were simply protecting your family the only way you knew how. Besides, don't forget that in finding Jeff, we also gave a name to the man who's trying to take him down. I would lay odds that, as we speak, something else is in the works to find this Simon character."

"You're right," East said.

"How will you get *Baby* home?" Ally asked.

"When Jeff is strong enough, we'll drive her home."

In spite of her determination not to do so, she started to cry.

"I feel like I'm losing you," she whispered.

East took her in his arms. "Never," he said softly. "You know where I am. When you're ready, just come back to me. That's all I ask."

"Oh, I'll be there," Ally said. "For as long as you'll let me."

East cupped her face, swiping at a slow stream of her tears with the balls of his thumbs.

"Forever sounds good to me," he said.

"Is that a proposal?"

"Did you by any chance happen to memorize that *Kama Sutra* thing?" he asked.

She managed to grin. "Most of it, I imagine."

"Then by the time you come back, have the rest of it put to memory. It will be something to look forward to on our wedding night."

"I love you, East."

"And I love you, too," he said softly. "Hurry home to me."

It was nightfall and the hospital sounds were far more subdued than they were during the day. East dozed in a chair by Jeff's bed, while compliments of Jonah, a guard stood watch outside the door. Until they were certain no more threats were forthcoming, they would assume nothing. All the information they'd learned about the Brotherhood's illicit activities had been given to Jonah—the rest of it was up to him.

Jeff shifted restlessly and East woke abruptly, moving to his bedside and laying his hand on Jeff's arm, then his forehead, testing for fever. To his relief, he was almost cool.

"Dad...is that you?"

East grinned. "Who did you think it would be...that woman you keep refusing to discuss?"

A faint smile slid across Jeff's face and then he closed his eyes, opening them again seconds later.

"I knew you'd come."

East curled his fingers around Jeff's forearm and gave it a quick squeeze.

"Thanks to your quick thinking. That little clue you dropped about crashing and burning was good. You know…if you ever decide to forego medical school, you'd make a hell of a good spy."

"Bite your damned tongue," Jeff mumbled.

East laughed softly.

"Did I dream it, or was there a woman with you?" Jeff asked.

Pain pierced East's composure. "No, you didn't dream her," East said. "Although I'll admit she's a dream of a lady."

The remark was so out of character for East that Jeff made himself focus.

"Sounds serious."

"Yeah," East said.

"Where is she?"

East looked away. "I don't know and that's the hell of it. Now get some sleep. I won't be far."

Jeff closed his eyes as East settled back in his chair. Just when East thought Jeff had fallen back to sleep, he slipped one last comment into the night.

"If she matters, she'll be back."

East didn't bother to open his eyes. "How do you know?"

"It's what I keep telling myself."

The loneliness in that single sentence made East sad. It was just as he'd suspected. There was, or at least there had been, someone special in his life.

As he stood, a soft knock sounded on the door. He looked up to see a nurse poke her head in the door.

"Mr. Kirby, there's a call for you in the waiting room."

He glanced at Jeff one last time, then headed for the door, leaving quick instructions with the guard that he'd be right back.

When he got to the waiting area, the phone was off the hook, and the room was empty. Hoping it was Ally, he answered.

"This is Easton Kirby."

"And a formidable opponent you were."

East's blood chilled. "You son of a bitch."

The man chuckled. "Yes, probably. However, that's not why I called."

"You leave me and my family alone, or so help me, God, I'll find you and—"

"There's no need for threats," he said sharply. "That's why I called. I misjudged you. I don't make the same mistakes twice. Rest assured that I will succeed in my mission, but that you will in no way be further involved."

"I wouldn't have been involved in the first place if you hadn't taken my son," East snapped.

"So I realized, but alas, too late. However, it's never too late to right a wrong, don't you agree?"

"There's nothing we could possibly agree upon. You won't get away with this, and I wish you straight to hell."

The man laughed again, only it was brief and bitter.

"But that's just the point, you see. I'm already there."

Epilogue

East walked out to the balcony of his apartment, eyeing the terrace below and making a mental note to have the hotel groundskeepers install some new lighting around the base of the railing. It seemed a little dim.

The television was playing in the room behind him, but he paid it no mind. It was just noise—something to keep him from thinking about how lonesome he really was. It had been a month yesterday since Jeff's rescue, and a month today since he'd last seen Ally. From the first day of his return, he'd awakened with the hope that she would call, or that he would have a letter from her in the mail. And each day that passed without that hope coming to fruition brought a deeper sense of pain to his life. He wouldn't let himself think that she'd come to harm on that last assignment. He made himself remember how cool and poised she'd been when she'd faced down the entire Brotherhood of Blood. She was a professional—and a damned smart one, he reminded himself. She wouldn't let herself get caught up in something she couldn't control.

But it had been thirty days—and thirty nights—and he hurt so deep inside his gut that he sometimes wondered if the pain would kill him after all. He missed her laughter and that prim, prissy look she got when her authority was questioned. He wanted to watch her eat waffles, one square at a time, and every hour of the day he would tell her that he loved her so that she wouldn't forget he wasn't like her parents—so she wouldn't forget the woman she'd become.

He braced his hands against the railing and leaned forward, absently watching the sunset. One moment it was there, hovering on the edge of the horizon, then disappearing so quickly that it seemed as if the ocean had suddenly opened its mouth and swallowed it whole. At once, a vivid streak of color spread upward from the horizon, painting the sky in varying shades of purple and pink.

"It's beautiful, isn't it?"

East spun. "Ally?"

"Is that offer still open?" she asked.

A wide grin split the somberness of his face. "Did you memorize the rest of that damned book?"

"Yes."

"Then yes, a thousand times yes, it's still open."

She returned the grin and then gasped as he lifted her off her feet and began kissing her over and over on every inch of her face. She closed her eyes, deciding that being loved by Easton Kirby was a little akin to flying—a little frightening, but well worth the ride.

A short while later, East was in the midst of explanations about Jeff's full recovery and return to his studies, when Ally decided it was time to share her own bit of news.

She cleared her throat and folded her hands in front of her, as if waiting for permission to speak.

When East saw her gathering herself, and then watched that beautiful mouth slightly purse, he grinned.

"Got something to say, have you?"

"How do you know?" she asked.

He shrugged, unwilling to give away the one thing he knew about her that might hold him in good stead for the next sixty or so years.

"Psychic, I guess. So what's up?"

"I brought you a present...two actually."

His grin widened. "I like presents. What are they?"

She headed for the bedroom, returning momentarily with a small, flat package and handed it to him.

East chuckled. It was a book, that much he knew. Expecting it to be a copy of that blessed *Kama Sutra,* he was taken aback by the pink and blue cover, as well as the title.

"What To Name Your Baby?"

She smiled primly. "Since it's our first, I thought you might like to choose. But if we have another, the pleasure will be mine, okay?"

The grin on his face started to slide as his eyes began to widen. Ally stared, watching in sudden fascination and wondering if one facial muscle was connected to another in such a way that what was happening was beyond East's control, or if he had gone into shock. She did a quick mental breakdown of the construction of the human form and decided upon the latter. It was definitely shock. But the longer he remained silent, the more she began to worry. Finally, she could stand the suspense no longer.

"Don't you have something to say?"

He stared at her face, then her belly, then back at her face again, blinking through a blur of quick tears.

"Actually, I think I have two," he mumbled.

This wasn't going exactly as she had planned. Her fingers knotted as she tried to offer a brief smile. It didn't come off as she'd wanted.

East saw the sudden terror in her eyes, but it was nothing to the joy in his heart.

He touched her belly, then his heart. "I don't think I've ever been so happy in my entire adult life."

Her lips parted in a quick, sweet smile.

"I'm so relieved. I mean, we hadn't discussed any of—"

"Will you marry me?"

The smile dissolved into full-fledged tears.

"Oh, East, I was hoping you would ask me that, since I've already turned in my resignation with SPEAR." She splayed her hands across the middle of her belly. "I mean…I can't be running all over the country anymore and endangering our child. I will never do to my baby, what my parents did to me. I will be there in the night when it cries. I will be there to see first steps and hear those precious first words. And I will die before I'll give this baby to someone else to raise."

He gathered her close to him, holding her as if she was the most precious thing on this earth, which to him, she was.

Her pledge had him speechless. Finally, he managed to mutter. "Why is it that a woman always cries when she's happy?"

She sniffed, taking the handkerchief he offered as she considered the question he'd unwittingly asked.

"You know, I think it has to do with an uneven level of hormones at the moment of excitement...or fear...as the case may be. In fact, I remember reading—"

He silenced her with another kiss, and then another, and then another. It was some time later before he thought to ask her again.

"You know, you never did answer my question. *Will* you marry me, Alicia Corbin, or are you going to ask me to live in sin?"

Her eyes widened in disbelief. Just when she started to explain why she would never do that, she realized he was grinning.

"You're teasing me now, aren't you?"

"Oh, yeah," he said softly.

An answering grin tilted the corners of her lips.

"Well, since I can't have the father of my children being any kind of a sinner, then I suppose I will have to say yes."

"Ah God, Ally, you have given me something I never thought I'd have," he said.

"You mean children?"

He shook his head, thinking back to the way he'd been before Jonah had sent her—living in limbo and guilt.

"No, I'm talking about my life. You not only gave my first son back to me, but you are giving me a future I never thought I'd have." He kissed her softly, then added. "So, thank you. Thank you so much for loving me."

Now her tears were coming in earnest. "It was easy," she said. "All I had to do was trust you enough to let go."

"I'll never let you fall," he promised.

"Oh, I know that."

East took her by the hand. "Let's go call Jeff."

She looked a little nervous.

"What will we say?"

"That he's getting a mother and a brother, all at the same time."

"I hope he doesn't resent me…us," she amended, thinking of the baby she was carrying.

"How could he resent the woman who helped save his life? Now come with me. I'm in the mood for spreading good news."

"Okay," she said. "But after that, I thought we might try out page forty-two tonight. It's a little complicated and I won't be able to do those kind of contortions once I start getting big."

East's eyes widened as he thought of her and that book all over again. Then he took her by the hand and led her toward the bedroom instead.

"We'll call Jeff tomorrow, now show me page forty-two."

It was far into the morning before East rose up on one elbow and gazed down at Ally, who lay sleeping beside him. He kept marveling at how someone could maintain such a level of naivete while filled with so much uninhibited passion. Finally, he leaned over, pressing a soft, butterfly kiss against her cheek, then whispering in her ear.

"Education is a wonderful thing."

*   *   *   *   *

Next month, look for

UNDERCOVER BRIDE

by Kylie Brant as
Intimate Moments' exciting

A YEAR OF LOVING DANGEROUSLY

series continues. Turn the page
for a sneak preview…

Chapter 1

He didn't look like a man committed to spreading hatred, prejudice and destruction.

Rachel Grunwald tacked the color 8×10 glossy on to the padded wall before her where she could study it while she continued her workout. The photo of Caleb Carpenter managed to convey an aura of power; an invisible energy that all but crackled just below the surface. Based on his physical appearance alone, she would have guessed the man as high-level military, or even as one of those exorbitantly priced motivational speakers who seemed to abound these days. As the leader of The Brotherhood of Blood, Carpenter was, in a manner of speaking, both.

She drew her arms up and slowly slid one foot behind her to rest on point. Eyes fixed dispassionately on the photo, she arched her back and raised her leg, the fluid movement as graceful as ballet.

Most would consider the man handsome. His piercing blue eyes contrasted sharply with his short, sleek black hair. Some might mistake the strength in his jaw as a mark of integrity; the squared off chin as a sign of determination. Few, she imagined, would look at the man and guess him a racist who preached death or deportation for the non-Aryan and disabled.

She spun, her foot shooting out to land hard against the picture. If Carpenter had actually been standing before her, she would have just broken his jaw. A slight frown marred her exquisite face. Her timing was off. She aimed for his nose. With an acquired patience, she ran through the move a dozen more times, until she was satisfied with it. In her eight years as an agent she'd found it most effective to endeavor to disarm an opponent completely.

She bent to the palm-size tape recorder on the floor, pressed Play, and waited for the quietly measured tones of a man she'd never met to describe her next mission.

"You've heard, I'm sure, about the rescue of East Kirby's son. I'm sorry to say we failed to apprehend the kidnapper."

The kidnapper, Rachel knew, was thought to be the same man attempting to destroy SPEAR, the agency she worked for, and the man at its helm, Jonah himself. She feinted right, then plowed her left fist into the long foam-packed punching bag, imaging for the moment it was the stomach of the traitor.

"Jeff Kirby was found buried alive on the Brotherhood of Blood compound in Idaho, which is owned and operated by Caleb Carpenter. A photo of him has been included. We need to discover the link between Simon and Carpenter. With your experience, of course, you're perfectly suited to do so."

The experience Jonah referred to was her specialty

at anti-militia assignments. Her most recent task had been to infiltrate Comrades, a white-supremacist group hidden deep in the Appalachian Mountains of northeastern Pennsylvania.

Panting, she moved away from the bag and grabbed one of the ropes that dangled from the overhead beams she'd left intact when she'd had the old barn renovated for her home. Scrambling up it, she kept her mind focused on the words coming from the machine, and off her straining muscles.

"Carpenter is said to be looking for a wife to complete his hold on the new union he's creating. I'll assume you'll have no difficulty arranging an introduction. And then, in convincing him that you are a woman worthy of bearing his seed to propagate his empire."

Having reached the top of the rope, Rachel heaved herself to sit astride the beam, then rose to balance, arms outstretched. "Sure, Jonah," she murmured, as she tiptoed the length of the beam. Constructing a pirouette, she crossed back to the rope and began her descent. "Pretend fiancée to a man handsome as sin who just happens to be Satan's counterpart? No problem."

"We know Carpenter's stated intention to unite all the militia groups in the nation into one army capable of taking down the U.S. government." Jonah's voice hardened. "I need details, Rachel. Who's he dealing with, and how does he hope to bring about the revolution? And finally, what tie does Simon have with the Brotherhood? His involvement, I'm certain, is critical."

She let go of the rope and dropped lightly to the floor. The tape was now silent, save for a faint whirring sound as its automatic destruction mechanism activated.

After she showered and ate dinner, she poured herself a glass of wine and sat down in the over-stuffed sofa in front of the fireplace. She let her mind drift, ideas half forming, to be analyzed, rejected, reformed. Rachel rested the cool side of the goblet against her cheek. It had ceased to seem ironic that she'd become as much a zealot for her beliefs as had her father, although their views could not be more diametrically opposed. She accepted the fact that had it not been for her miserable childhood, for her father, SPEAR would never have sought her out. She accepted that twist of fate, and poured everything she had into the agency, which represented all she believed in. Truth. Justice. Loyalty.

It certainly wouldn't be fate she'd rely on as she considered her new mission. It wouldn't be luck, either. She considered the best way to get close to Caleb Carpenter. Close enough to learn his secrets, to discover his strategy.

Close enough to destroy him.

USA *Today* Bestselling Author

SHARON
SALA

has won readers' hearts with thrilling tales
of romantic suspense. Now Silhouette Books
is proud to present five passionate stories from
this beloved author.

Available in August 2000:
ALWAYS A LADY
A beauty queen whose dreams have been dashed in a
tragic twist of fate seeks shelter for her wounded spirit
in the arms of a rough-edged cowboy....

Available in September 2000:
GENTLE PERSUASION
A brooding detective risks everything to protect the
woman he once let walk away from him....

Available in October 2000:
SARA'S ANGEL
A woman on the run searches desperately for a reclusive
Native American secret agent—the only man who can save
her from the danger that stalks her!

Available in November 2000:
HONOR'S PROMISE
A struggling waitress discovers she is really a rich heiress—
and must enter a powerful new world of wealth and
privilege on the arm of a handsome stranger....

Available in December 2000:
KING'S RANSOM
A lone woman returns home to the ranch where she was
raised, and discovers danger—as well as the man she once
loved with all her heart....

Look Who's Celebrating Our 20th Anniversary:

Celebrate 20 YEARS

"In 1980, Silhouette gave a home to my first book and became my family. Happy 20th Anniversary! And may we celebrate twenty more."

—*New York Times* bestselling author
Nora Roberts

"Twenty years of Silhouette! I can hardly believe it. Looking back on it, I find that my life and my books for Silhouette were inextricably intertwined.... Every Silhouette I wrote was a piece of my life. So, thank you, Silhouette, and may you have many more anniversaries."

—International bestselling author
Candace Camp

"Twenty years publishing fiction by women, for women, and about women is something to celebrate! I am honored to be a part of Silhouette's proud tradition— one that I have no doubt will continue being cherished by women the world over for a long, long time to come."

—International bestselling author
Maggie Shayne

INTIMATE MOMENTS®
Silhouette®

MAITLAND MATERNITY

Where the luckiest babies are born!

Join Harlequin® and Silhouette® for a special 12-book series about the world-renowned Maitland Maternity Clinic, owned and operated by the prominent Maitland family of Austin, Texas, where romances are born, secrets are revealed…and bundles of joy are delivered!

Look for

MAITLAND MATERNITY

titles at your favorite retail outlet, starting in August 2000

HARLEQUIN®
Makes any time special™

Silhouette®
Where love comes alive™

Coming Soon
Silhouette Books presents

Weddings in White

(on sale September 2000)

A 3-in-1 keepsake collection
by international bestselling author

DIANA PALMER

Three heart-stoppingly handsome bachelors are paired
up with three innocent beauties who long to marry the
men of their dreams. This dazzling collection showcases
the enchanting characters and searing passion that
has made Diana Palmer a legendary talent
in the romance industry.

Unlikely Lover:
Can a feisty secretary and a gruff oilman fight
the true course of love?

The Princess Bride:
For better, for worse, starry-eyed Tiffany Blair captivated
Kingman Marshall's iron-clad heart....

Callaghan's Bride:
Callaghan Hart swore marriage was for fools—until
Tess Brady branded him with her sweetly seductive kisses!

Available at your favorite retail outlet.

Silhouette®
Where love comes alive™

ATTENTION,
LINDSAY McKENNA FANS!

**Morgan Trayhern has three brand-new missions
in Lindsay McKenna's latest series:**

**Morgan's men are made for battle—
but are they ready for love?**

The excitement begins in July 2000, with
Lindsay McKenna's 50th book!

MAN OF PASSION
(Silhouette Special Edition® #1334)
Featuring rugged Rafe Antonio, aristocrat by birth,
loner by choice. But not for long....

Coming in November 2000:

A MAN ALONE
(Silhouette Special Edition® #1357)
Featuring Thane Hamilton, a wounded war hero on his way
home to the woman who has always secretly loved him....

*Look for the third book in the series in early 2001! In the
meantime, don't miss Lindsay McKenna's brand-new,
longer-length single title, available in August 2000:*

MORGAN'S MERCENARIES:
HEART OF THE WARRIOR

Only from Lindsay McKenna and
Silhouette Books!

Celebrate
Silhouette's 20th Anniversary
with *New York Times* bestselling author

LINDA HOWARD

and get reacquainted with the Mackenzie family in

Test pilot Joe "Breed" Mackenzie was on a

MACKENZIE'S MISSION

dangerous mission, and he wasn't about to let sexy civilian Caroline Evans—a woman who looked too good and knew too much—get in his way....

On sale in July 2000

And don't miss the brand-new, long-awaited story of Chance Mackenzie in

A GAME OF CHANCE,

Intimate Moments #1021
On sale in August 2000

Available at your favorite retail outlet

COMING NEXT MONTH

#1021 A GAME OF CHANCE—Linda Howard

Hot on the trail of a suspected terrorist, covert intelligence officer Chance Mackenzie found, seduced and subtly convinced the man's daughter, Sunny Miller, to lead her father out of hiding. The plan worked, but then Sunny discovered the truth behind Chance's so-called affections. Now the agent who *always* got his man had to figure out a way to get his woman.

#1022 UNDERCOVER BRIDE—Kylie Brant
A Year of Loving Dangerously

SPEAR agent Rachel Grunwald knew that her assignment to pose as a potential wife for white supremacist leader Caleb Carpenter didn't allow for any mistakes. But if Caleb was so evil, why did her heart skip a beat whenever he was around? Was it possible that Caleb had a secret agenda of his own?

#1023 BLADE'S LADY—Fiona Brand

For nearly twenty years, SAS soldier Blade Lombard had dreamed of nothing but Anna Tarrant. And now, here she stood, in the flesh—and in desperate need of Blade's help. She was on the run and out of time, and if Blade didn't answer her call, the woman of his dreams would disappear into the night—forever.

#1024 GABRIEL'S HONOR—Barbara McCauley
Secrets!

For months, Melanie Hart's life, and that of her four-year-old, had been threatened by the very people who were supposed to love them. Forced to go into hiding, Melanie hadn't counted on Gabriel Sinclair coming to her rescue. Could she trust the rugged loner with everything she held most dear—including her love?

#1025 THE LAWMAN AND THE LADY—Pat Warren

From the moment detective Nick Bennett was assigned to protect her, he couldn't get sexy single mom Tate Monroe off his mind. But with Tate's and her son's lives in danger, Nick *had* to focus on their safety—not on Tate's stunning beauty. Once the threat was over, though, Nick had his sights set on winning Tate's heart....

#1026 SHOTGUN BRIDE—Leann Harris

As the heiress to her father's fortune, Renee Girouard was in serious danger. Her only chance at survival was to marry lawman Matthew Hawkins and pretend to live happily ever after. But a marriage of convenience didn't guarantee she wouldn't feel anything for her brooding protector—especially when he kept risking his life to save hers.

CMN0700